FEASTING the WOLF

FEASTING the WOLF

SUSAN PRICE

USBORNE

Editorial Consultant: Tony Bradman

First published in the UK in 2007 by Usborne Publishing Ltd.,
Usborne House, 83-85 Saffron Hill, London EC1N 8RT, England. www.usborne.com

Text copyright © Susan Price, 2007

Map copyright © Usborne Publishing Ltd., 2007

Cover photography: the Vendel helmet can be seen in the Gold Room in
The Museum of National Antiquities, Stockholm, Sweden.

Map by Juliet Percival.

The name Usborne and the devices ♈ ⊕ are Trade Marks of
Usborne Publishing Ltd.

A CIP catalogue record for this book is available from the British Library.

JFMAMJJ SOND/07   ISBN 9780746077009   Printed in Great Britain.

Shetland
Lerwick

NORWAY

Orkney

PICTLAND

NORTHUMBRIA
Carlisle   Lindisfarne
            River Tyne
CUMBRIA   York   DANELAND
IRELAND
Dublin
        MERCIA
        EAST ANGLIA

WESSEX

Paris

N

FRANKLAND

W   E

S

CHAPTER ONE

Geese Going South

THE AXE SMASHED DOWN on the shield, the force of the blow driving Ketil's raised arm into his face and buckling his knees under him. The inner side of his shield hit his head. Splinters flew. He yelled, "Hold! Hold!"

Ottar laughed, and laid on harder, yelling, "You shall feed the ravens!"

Ketil tried to stand under the blows, but they pounded down too fast. He saw splinters of wood, hacked from his shield, falling around him. Soon there'd be no shield left to protect him from the axe's edge. He gave up and fell to the ground, holding the shield above him, trying to curl up under its shelter.

"Ha!" Ottar smashed down another blow. "Feast the wolf!" He backed off, panting, stooping to lean on his knees.

Ulfbjorn sat nearby, with folded arms, on an upturned bucket. He laughed at them both.

When Ottar had a little breath back, he looked and saw that Ketil was still trying to hide his big body and long legs under his shield. He laughed too. Laughing and panting, he said, "You can come out now!"

"I'm dead," Ketil said. "Go away and stop bothering me!"

Ulfbjorn got up and walked over to them. He kicked Ketil's leg gently and said, "In a real battle, you would be dead. You've got to be quicker, Ketil. You want to look round and watch the grass grow – but there's no time for that in battle."

Ketil rolled and sat up, his hacked shield held before him. He grinned up at his uncle. "Ah, but if we're ever in a real battle, I shall put on my bearskin and run berserk." The War God, Odin, was supposed to send his followers mad with battle-frenzy. They were even supposed to put on bearskin shirts, turn into bears, and fight with the strength of bears.

"What if Odin doesn't come to you?" Ulfbjorn said.

Ketil clambered to his feet, a long-legged, long-faced lad with light brown hair. He was as tall as Ulfbjorn, and a head taller than Ottar. "I promise you, Uncle, when I come among the enemy, their dead will number more than their living."

"Be serious," Ottar said. "If you won't be serious, we'll never be any good." Ottar was wiry, with a small, neat round head. His hair, brows and lashes were all very dark, though his eyes were light grey. He took after his Pictish mother. It offended him that Ketil treated their weapons-practice as a game. Ottar wanted to be the best at axe-play and swordplay, the best there was, and that meant practising and practising. But Ketil wouldn't practise at all if Ottar didn't make him. He said to Ulfbjorn, "Tell him to be serious."

"If we went up to the house now," Ketil said, "I wonder if we could get something to eat?"

"Ketil!" Ottar said.

Ketil laughed and kicked aside the remains of his

shield. It had only been a practice one – a few pieces of wood nailed together, with straps and grips made of rope. Good enough to be battered to flinders in a game. In one of the farm's storehouses, he had a real shield – nothing fancy, but a good, strong shield, fit for battle. He had an axe, too, and a spear, a bow and twenty-four arrows, just as the law said every free man should have, in case the King of Norway called on him to fight. Ulfbjorn had given him the war-gear on his twelfth birthday, when he'd become a man; and it was mostly Ulfbjorn who'd taught him and Ottar to use them. "Don't fret, Ottar," Ketil said. "We've plenty of time. How long has the Army been pestering the Saxons now? Five years?"

"Nine!" Ottar said. He thought Ketil should know that.

"Nine! Well, they're going to hang around while we get something to eat, then, aren't they, Cod-Face?"

"Aye," Ulfbjorn said. "Let's go and get something to eat."

Ketil and Ulfbjorn started back to the house. Ottar stayed where he was. He called after them, "We'll come back and practise afterwards!"

"It'll be dark," Ketil said, over his shoulder.

"We'll practise tomorrow then!" Ottar said.

Ketil threw back his head and groaned. Weapons-practice was all right now and again – and the law said a man had to be able to use his weapons – but honestly, Ottar thought about nothing else lately. It was becoming a bore.

"You have to eat," Ulfbjorn said. "Keep your strength up! Grow a bit taller!"

Ottar was stung by that reference to his height – but the light was dimming, and he was hungry. He followed them.

It was late summer, still warm, and the sheep were in the hills. Only the farm's five strong little northern horses were penned in the home-field. They came trotting over. "I've nothing for you," Ketil said to them, but he stopped to rub noses with them.

Ottar, catching up, said to Ulfbjorn, "They call it 'the Great Army', don't they?" If he had to give up weapons-practice, then he would get Ulfbjorn to talk about his favourite subject. And he loved to roll the words "Great Army" over his tongue. "Why's that?"

"Because it's the biggest army ever seen," Ulfbjorn said. "More men than anybody could count. Hundreds and hundreds."

Ottar's heart swelled at the thought of that. Imagine being one of them! Knowing yourself to be part of the greatest army ever! "And it's led by Halfdan?" he asked – though he knew perfectly well who the Army's leaders were. Ketil guessed his game, and was grinning at him. Ottar ignored him.

"There's more than one leader," Ulfbjorn said. "Halfdan's one – then there's Guthrum – and Ivar, before he died. There are others, but those are the ones I've heard of."

"Dad says they're nothing but Vikings – just pirates and raiders," Ketil said, and laughed when Ottar frowned. He'd known that would irritate him.

"He's not far wrong," Ulfbjorn said. "They're outlaws – or younger sons with no land to call their own – or men who just want to grab some loot and land."

It all sounded fine to Ottar. If you were born a younger son, with no land, you could accept that you'd be poor all your life – or you could join the Great Army, and fight, make yourself famous and win gold. And when you came home, you could buy the family farm from your brothers, if you wanted to be bothered.

"And *was* it nine years ago they first came?" Ottar asked. He knew it was.

"Aye... Well, when they first came to the Saxon lands." He meant the lands far to the south, even south of Pictland. "They'd been across the sea before that, raiding over there. In Frankland. There's a big city over there, called Paris. They besieged that."

"Where did they first come?" Ottar asked. "Was it Wessex?"

"No, not Wessex!" Ulfbjorn said. "Wessex is strong. They came to East Anglia – that's ten, fourteen days' sailing from here." Even Ketil looked impressed by so great a distance. "Before that they'd been even further south, down in the Frankish lands, getting gold, horses – drinking wine, not ale, wine."

Ottar shook his head wonderingly, his eyes wide. It was his secret ambition that, one day, he would serve a king, as one of the king's fighting men. He would be a great warrior and the king would reward him with horses and gold, and give him a beautiful noblewoman for his wife – maybe even one of the king's own daughters. And he'd come back home to Shetland to visit. In his own ship. And he'd ride to visit Ketil and Ulfbjorn on his prancing horse and – he'd give them great gifts, to show he remembered them.

"The Army came over to East Anglia," Ulfbjorn said, "because all the Saxon kings are too busy fighting each other to get an army together to fight anybody else. So, easy pickings. It wasn't East Anglia the Army were after, though – it was York. They just made winter quarters in East Anglia, and took horses – they're famous for their horses there."

Ottar's eyes shone, as he imagined horses with arched necks and coats shining like silk – rich men's horses. To win one in battle was far more glorious than buying it.

"They moved up to York the next year," Ulfbjorn said. He knew, because he'd been trading himself, to York, and across the North Sea to Hathaby in Daneland, and he'd picked up all the news. Often, when ships put into their Shetland port of Lerwick, he'd go along and gossip with the shipmen, and learn what was going on in the world. "Some went in ships and some went by horse. There are these stone roads in the Saxon lands, built time out of mind by the Roman giants. You can make good speed along them. They came at York by land

and sea, in the early winter, and they walked in. Took it without a fight."

Ottar gave a little skip as they walked. He loved hearing this sort of talk. "The Saxons don't know how to fight!"

"The Saxons were fighting each other," Ketil said. "Isn't that right?"

Ulfbjorn nodded. "That's why Ivar and Halfdan took the Army there. They knew that while all the Saxon leaders were fighting each other, not one of them could get enough men together to fight them. It was a Saxon feast day as well – they were holding a fair and drinking. The last thing they expected was to be attacked."

"Ha!" Ottar said, and cut short the life of some nettles with his axe.

"That was what, eight years ago?" Ulfbjorn said. "You and Ketil were just wee lads. Since then Halfdan and Ivar have been roaming about with their men, up and down through the Saxon lands, through Mercia and back to East Anglia, and into Wessex. The Christians have these 'monasteries' where their holy men live, and they have dishes of gold and silver, and gold candlesticks, and bits of dead people in boxes of gold studded all over with gemstones – Ivar and Halfdan put all that in their treasury. And slaves, they took slaves – sold 'em in Dublin and Hathaby. Good pickings."

They reached the farmyard, which was paved with flat stones, so that people didn't have to wade through deep muck and mud in wet weather. They came to the storehouses first, and stopped to duck inside, and hang their axes on the pegs driven into the stone walls.

Beside the storehouses was a little smithy, where farm tools could be made and repaired; and a bathhouse. The farmhouse was on the other side of the paved yard, beside the stable and the byre. All of these buildings were long and low, with stone walls and turf roofs. Smoke drifted from the smoke-hole of the house.

"Ivar died about a year ago," Ulfbjorn said, as they came out of the storehouse. "Things changed a bit then. The Army split up."

"King Halfdan came north, didn't he?" Ottar said.

"King?" Ulfbjorn said. "He calls himself 'king'. His brother's the King of Daneland, but he's no king."

"Halfdan made himself a king!" Ottar said. "By fighting! By being the best – by winning gold!"

"By feasting the wolf and raven," Ulfbjorn said, and laughed. Wolves and ravens came to eat the dead after a battle, so that was the way poets described battle – *spreading a feast before the wolf and raven*. "But aye, Halfdan brought his part of the Army north, while Guthrum took his men south. Halfdan came up into Northumbria – there's a lot of monasteries and gold in that part of the country. He's making his winter quarters on the river Tyne, I hear."

"Gold," Ottar said. He looked at the farm around him. It was a well-kept, comfortable farm, and he envied Ketil for being the only son of his family to inherit it. He, Ottar, was the third of three brothers, and if his father split the land between the three of them, none of them would have enough to live on. If he gave all the land to his eldest son, then Ottar and his other brother would have none – unless they could somehow earn gold enough to buy some. Or win such favour with a king that the king gifted them gold and farms.

Of course, it wasn't just the land and the buildings that made Ketil's home so comfortable.

Three days before, Ottar had been at his own farm, and his mother had learned that he was going to visit Ketil for a few days. She'd been furious. She disliked him going, because she missed his company.

"Oh, aye, it's a rich, comfortable farm," she'd said. "Why wouldn't it be? They came in from the sea and took the land. They didn't have to serve a chief for it. They didn't break their backs clearing stones and carrying basket after basket of seaweed up from the beach to dig into the fields. They stole land that had already been worked over, the heathens!" She'd been banging about in her kitchen among her Pictish slaves and servants, speaking her own language.

Ottar's father, Harald, had been sitting in the hall, on the other side of the leather curtain that screened hall and kitchen from each other. Harald was a Northman, and a heathen. His grandfather had come by ship from Norway, and had taken land in Shetland. According to Harald, there hadn't been much fighting. "If the Picts let us alone, we let them alone," he said. "If there was fighting, they started it. We only wanted to farm."

Hearing his wife's words, he'd shouted out, in Norse, "Shut up, you old witch!" All his men, and Ottar's brothers, had laughed. Harald understood

Pictish, though he never spoke it except when giving orders to slaves. He always spoke Norse to his wife and children.

Ottar thought Ketil lucky because his mother and father were both Norwegian Shetlanders. They worshipped the same Gods and spoke the same language, though they could both speak a little Pictish when they had to speak to slaves or other natives who'd never learned Norwegian. Ketil's home wasn't divided between Pict and Northman, Christian and heathen, and was much calmer and happier for it. Ottar liked to spend time with Ketil, away from the pot-banging, the shouting and the crying at home. His mother always wanted him to be Pictish, and he couldn't be. Whatever she said, he was half-Northman.

"We should join the Army," Ottar said to Ketil. "Go and get us some gold. And when we've fought in some battles, we can take service with the King of Norway."

Ketil laughed.

"We should!" Ottar said. "Do you just want to stay at home your whole life? Ulfbjorn went travelling – we should go, shouldn't we, Ulfbjorn?"

"You should travel while you're young," Ulfbjorn

said. "See a bit of the world beyond the farm walls, have some adventures… And it's better to be rich than poor in this world, that's a sure thing."

"See?" Ottar said. "Ulfbjorn thinks we should go!"

Ketil laughed. "One day." As they crossed the yard, they could look between the buildings and see the hayfield, with its rows of hayricks that everyone had worked so hard over. Further down the slopes were the fields where the barley and oats had been grown. The last sheaves had been brought into the barn only a few days before. Some other men could be seen down there, taking stones from the walls, to make gaps, so the animals could get in to graze on the stubble, and also manure the ground. And beyond those fields were the paths leading down to the beach, and the racks where they dried fish.

Ketil came to a stop and stood staring. Ottar went on a step or two, following Ulfbjorn, but then turned, wondering why his friend wasn't with him.

Ketil was looking out over the green hills, and the grey stone walls; at the white and yellow of the stubble-fields; and at the blue sky over all. The wind brought him a scent of grass, and heather-bells and sea. He drew in a deep breath, and felt a deep, wordless contentment rooting him to the ground; his ground.

"Come on," Ottar said, and Ketil dragged his feet, and his heart, from the spot, and they went on towards the house.

They were nearing the door when a cry from overhead made them look up. "Geese!" Ottar said. A big V of wild geese was flying overhead, honking, as they made their way south, to Pictland, for the winter. "The wind's from the north!"

It was the wind that would carry a ship southwards, towards the Saxon lands, where the Great Army was winning fame and gold. Ketil shook his head, and ducked in through the house door, into the dimness, the smoke, heat and smell of food.

Ottar remained outside, looking up, watching the geese, and wishing he was going with them.

Chapter Two
Wave Strider

THEY SAILED INTO LERWICK'S muddy bay, taking down their boat's little sail as they lost the wind, and rowing towards the shore. "There she is!" Ottar pointed. "That'll be her."

There was a ship beached at a distance from the settlement, her mast lowered. She wasn't the biggest ship they'd ever seen, but she was built for crossing oceans fast – long, slim, and high-sided. The strakes of her hull were painted red and black, in long stripes from her prow to her stern.

"What a beauty!" Ottar said. "I bet she flies!"

They'd been out fishing in the bay below Ketil's farm. Winter was coming, with its storms, and there wouldn't be many more opportunities to fish. A neighbour had rowed his boat close by theirs, and had yelled the news that there was a ship from Norway in at Lerwick. News would be as welcome at home as fresh fish, so the boys had sailed round to Lerwick, to find out all they could.

They beached their boat, jumping out onto the sand and hauling her up where the sea couldn't take her. Then they ran to look at the bigger ship. As they admired her, they were joined by a man in clothes of salt-stained grey wool. He came close and stood watching them with folded arms. He said, "You won't run off with our ship, lads, will you?"

They laughed. Ottar said, "Are you the Norway ship?"

The man put one hand on his chest. "Me? I'm not a ship. You can tell by my legs. But this ship, aye, this ship's from Norway, from the West Fjords."

"I'm Ottar Haraldssen, and this—"

"I'm Ketil Arnassen," said Ketil, who could speak for himself.

The man held out his right hand, and clasped theirs

23

briefly. "I'm Bjorn Bjornssen, of the fellowship of *Wave Strider*, and I'm glad to meet you."

"Is *Wave Strider* the ship's name?" Ottar asked. "She's beautiful!"

Bjorn nodded, pleased. "She's a great ship – she'll outrun a gale."

Ketil didn't want to listen to him boasting about the ship, so he quickly asked, "Are you trading?" Bjorn looked at him blankly. "Have you got timber? My father's interested in timber."

"Away!" Bjorn said. "With a ship like this! We're not traders!" He leaned towards Ketil. "We're war-makers! On our way to join Halfdan on the Tyne, and make war on the Saxons."

Ottar was so amazed and delighted he couldn't speak.

"But maybe we could trade, at that," Bjorn said. "You been fishing?"

Before Ketil could speak, Ottar had agreed to give all their fish to the *Wave Strider*'s crew, and Bjorn was shouting for men to come and fetch the catch.

The men came from the village of skin tents around the ship. They were all bearded, and some wore gold and silver armbands, or strings of amber, to show their wealth. Soon Ketil and Ottar's little boat was empty, and fish were cooking over the fires. The smell brought another man out of his tent. He shambled over to the fire, rubbing at his hair, which was all over the place. Seeing Ketil and Ottar, he stared at them from large grey eyes in a long horse-face. He said, rudely, "Who're you?" Looking round, he demanded, "Who're they?"

"They brought us these fish," Bjorn said. Looking at the boys, he added, "This is our shipmaster, Eyulf."

Ottar, and even Ketil, looked at him with interest. Ottar wanted to see what sort of great man could be master of such a ship. Ketil wondered what sort of man could be causing him such trouble and loss of fish.

Eyulf was lanky, with reddened, weathered skin, and brown hair. He wore work clothes in the greys and blacks of undyed wool, dirty, crumpled and salt-stained, but he had gold bands on his arms and fingers. "If you brought us food, you can stay," Eyulf said.

"They *gave* us food," Bjorn said. "Gave us all the fish they'd caught."

Eyulf stared at them for an eye's-blink, smiled and took a ring from his finger. "Friends should exchange gifts," he said, and held out the ring to Ketil.

Ketil took it, and turned it in his fingers. It was a simple ring, made of two wires twisted together, but it was gold, he was sure. It was so bright, so untouched by the salt that had marked Eyulf's clothes, that it could only be gold.

"Thanks shall you have!" he said.

"No thanks needed," Eyulf said. "An exchange of gifts between friends. Bjorn! Have you nothing for the other lad?"

Bjorn started, as if alarmed, and from a pouch at his belt took another ring and gave it to Ottar. It was silver, a little blackened, with a small chip of amber set in it – much less valuable than Ketil's ring, but Ottar was thrilled. Eyulf must be a rich lord, he thought, to give so generously in return for a few fish. It was an omen, telling him that his future was, indeed, full of kings rewarding him richly for his service.

Eyulf was stooping over the men who were grilling fish on sticks. "Come on, that's done! Guests first, then me." To Ottar and Ketil he said, "Let's eat."

They sat on the ground by the fires, breathing the

smell of burning turf and driftwood, with the wind blowing gusts of sparks at them. They ate hot fish, and groats that had been long stewing in the crews' pots; and drank beer that the crew had bought from the township. It was strong stuff, and soon loosened tongues. Ottar laughed a lot, his face flushed, marvelling that he was sitting there, with men who were on their way to join the Great Army. Even Ketil began to feel at ease, especially when the men started swapping tales of their travels, laughing and trying to outdo each other.

There were men who had been on trading trips, where they'd had to defend their cargos against Viking-pirates; and men who'd been on raids into Ireland and the Hebrides; and men who'd fought with the Great Army before – some in England, and some on the Continent. There were stories of storms, and shipwrecks, and ambushes, and gold.

There were men who had scars to show, and could tell where and when and how they'd received the wounds; and how ill they'd been – almost dying – before recovering. There were men who could show gold armbands, or rings, and tell how and where they'd won them. Ottar felt he was feasting with heroes.

"We can fight," he burst out. "Ketil and me. We've been practising. We want to join the Army too."

Ketil felt like burying himself in the sand. He and Ottar were so soft and scrawny beside these full-grown, scarred, hairy men, who'd fought in real battles – not merely in play fights against their friends.

But although the men around them laughed, it didn't sound as if they thought Ottar's notion worthless.

"How old are you?" Bjorn asked.

Ketil hung his head, unwilling to talk, but Ottar said, "Six-years-and-ten!" It was a lie. They wouldn't turn six-and-ten until Sun Month, and it was only Leaf-Fall Month now.

The men nodded – the boys looked that old. "You're a bit scrawny," Eyulf said to Ottar, "but your friend's a well-built lad."

"I'm as strong as he is!" Ottar said. He didn't like people noticing that, although they were the same age, Ketil was taller and stronger-looking.

"Pulling on oars would soon put some muscle on him!" Bjorn said, and there was more laughter. Ottar clenched his fists, to show off his arm muscles, and laughed too.

Eyulf said, "I wasn't that old when I went on my first voyage. What do you know about boats?"

Ottar said, "We sailed here – we were out fishing when we heard about you! We're always in boats – we know all about boats! Don't we, Ketil?"

Ketil shrugged. The men were laughing at them again, and he wanted to go home.

"Are you seasick?" Eyulf asked.

"Never!"

Eyulf stared at Ottar. "We're going further than across the bay. If you start chucking your guts up when we're out in the North Sea, your mother won't be on board!"

More laughter. "We're never sick!" Ottar said. "Are we, Ketil?"

"Don't know," Ketil muttered. The truth was, he'd never been out of sight of the Shetland shore. He didn't know how he would feel on a ship t he size of *Wave Strider*, in the open sea.

"Can you fight?" Eyulf asked.

Ottar nodded eagerly. He'd never been far out to sea either, and he'd never fought, except practice fights against Ketil and Ulfbjorn; but he was sure that, if Eyulf only gave him the chance, he could sail across the sea, and he could kill Saxons. He had to, if he wanted to serve a king, and be rich.

A man who hadn't spoken yet jumped up. He was lightly built, but wiry and strong, with dark hair hanging over his brow, and cut short at his shoulders. "Let's see what they can do."

There were cheers, and laughter, from the men, who all got up. Some formed a rough circle, while others darted away to fetch things. Someone handed Ottar a shield, saying, "Up!"

Ottar got up, slowly, unsure of what was going on. Ketil watched in dismay, not knowing how to help.

The dark, wiry man, who others were calling "Hrolf", had found a thick, solid length of wood, as long as his forearm. He gestured Ottar towards him, then pointed his stick of wood at Ketil. "You next."

Ottar looked over his shoulder at Ketil, but then turned and faced Hrolf. Now he didn't feel so sure that he could fight, even though Hrolf was only one man. The crew of the *Wave Strider* surrounded them, all eagerly watching, and Ottar felt smaller, feebler and more like a child than he had for years. The shield he held was a real shield, with a boss and edging of iron, and an iron grip. It was much heavier than the practice shields he was used to –

and Hrolf was watching him come on with a wicked, threatening grin.

Ottar managed to get the shield on his arm, as his father and Ulfbjorn had taught him – but before he felt ready, Hrolf sprang forward and swept the stick of wood at his legs.

Ottar thought his leg was broken. He cried out in pain and tried to drop the shield – but his arm and hand were caught up in the strap and grip, and the heavy shield banged its iron rim against his legs instead. He stumbled and fell in the sand, and all around him went up a great jeering laugh. That laughter stung like saltwater in a cut.

"Now you," Hrolf said to Ketil, pointing at him with his stick of wood.

Ketil came up from the sand in a temper, hating the way these men had made a fool of his friend. He went over to Ottar, helped him up, and took the shield from him, but mostly he kept his eyes on Hrolf.

Ottar cleared out of the way. As Ketil put his arm through the strap and closed his fist around the grip, he was glaring at Hrolf, who grinned back. "I want a stick too," Ketil said.

"Ooh!" The noise went up from the crew in a

mocking whoop, mocking both Ketil and Hrolf. Someone handed Ketil a stick similar to Hrolf's. Ketil didn't see who. His eyes were on Hrolf.

They faced each other, circling slowly. Hrolf was still grinning, still sure of winning, but wary. Ketil was remembering all he'd learned. Hrolf would probably strike at his legs, in which case he had to jump; or he'd strike at his head, in which case he'd have to get the heavy shield up. Legs or head? He'd gone for Ottar's legs – did that mean he was more likely to go for Ketil's head?

Why am I waiting for him to move? Ketil thought; and ran forward, swinging as hard a blow as he could at Hrolf's head.

Hrolf jumped backwards, and Ketil's stick hit his shield – a jarring contact that boomed like a drum on the wood and clanged on the iron. The jar struck up Ketil's arm and rattled his teeth.

Ketil jumped back, and would have run in again, but he glimpsed the stick swinging for his legs. He jumped, desperately bringing up his long legs, so that the blow would pass under him. But he timed it wrong. He landed, stumbling, in the sand, and the stick still hit him, above the knee.

Ketil half fell, catching himself on his right arm,

the stick in his right hand. He glimpsed Hrolf's stick high above him against the sky, coming down for his head, and got his shield up. The blow crashed on the shield, booming, ringing, and crushed him and the shield down into the sand.

Men were cheering – cheering for Hrolf. Hrolf had won.

Ketil sat up. His shield-arm felt wrenched.

A big, square brown hand was stuck in front of his face. Someone was offering him a hand up. It was Hrolf.

"He's good!" Hrolf called out, speaking to Eyulf. The grip of Hrolf's hand was tight, and he brought Ketil to his feet with one strong pull. "Too slow – but he'll get better."

"Have you weapons?" Eyulf asked. He was looking at Ketil, but it was Ottar who answered.

"We are men!" he said. "We've got shields and an axe each and leather hats –"

Eyulf held up a hand.

" – and leather shirts, and spears – "

Eyulf grinned. "All right – enough!"

" – and bows! With arrows!" Ottar finished.

"And do you still want to join me?" Eyulf asked.

"Aye!" Ottar said. "We do, Ketil, don't we?"

Ketil said nothing.

"Go and get your war-gear then," Eyulf said. "Be back with it before we sail, and you can join us. But maybe we'll be gone before you get here!"

Ottar grabbed Ketil by the shoulder, turned him, and hustled him down the beach towards their boat. He shouted back, over his shoulder, "We'll be here!"

Laughter followed them.

CHAPTER THREE

Leaving Home

THE WIND WAS AGAINST THEM going back, and they had to row. All the way, Ottar thought about what his life would be if he missed this chance. Stuck here on these narrow islands, the landless younger brother. He would spend all his days working for his brothers or begging them for favours. Unbearable! As they beached the boat in their home bay, he said, "We have to go!"

"You can go," Ketil said.

"When we made ourselves brothers, we said we'd go together!"

When they'd become men, at the age of twelve, they'd sworn a vow of blood-brothership. Ulfbjorn had told them how.

They'd gone up to the moors, with one of Ketil's spears. With his knife, Ottar had cut a long strip of turf, leaving it attached to the earth at one end. They'd propped up the free end on the spear, and had taken turns to crawl under it. Ottar went first, because he was the eldest.

Then they'd cut their palms, and let the blood drip onto the bare earth. Ottar had said, "Let the Gods witness our new birth as brothers, who will always defend, and help, and avenge each other."

They'd put the turf back into place, so it would grow into the earth again, sealing in their blood for ever.

"Aye, we're brothers," Ketil said now. "But when I said I'd come with you, we were only going trading to York, like Ulfbjorn. Then I was going to marry one of your sisters, and you were going to marry one of mine, and we were going to farm. I never said I wanted to join the Army!"

"But those were little boys' plans!" Ottar said. "I've got bigger ideas now! Better ideas!"

"Bigger, not better," Ketil said. "Look – we'll

always be brothers and stand by one another, but – brothers don't have to do everything the other one does."

"We were always going to go together!" Ottar said. They stood on the beach in the thickening dark, in silence. If Ketil stayed at home, Ottar saw, they wouldn't be friends any more when he returned from the Army – not friends like they were now. Ottar would have seen foreign lands, and faced danger, standing shoulder to shoulder with new friends in the shield-wall while the axe-music played. Ketil would have been ploughing, sowing and fishing. When Ketil talked about crops, Ottar wouldn't be interested; and when Ottar talked about battle, Ketil wouldn't understand. "We have to go together!" he said.

Ketil sighed. "You'd better sleep with us the night."

"No," Ottar said. "I've got to get my gear." He scrambled away through the deepening dusk towards his homeward path.

Ketil, left alone, thought of refusing to go. He had sworn to be Ottar's brother, but had never vowed that he would go to war with him. So he wouldn't be breaking a vow.

Ottar would think he had – and he would lose Ottar's friendship and his family's friendship. It was important to have friends, who would help you if harvests failed, or if you were attacked.

When Ottar had started going on about joining the Army a couple of years ago, Ketil had joined in, thinking it a game. By the time he'd realized that Ottar was serious, Ottar thought that Ketil shared his ambition. Ketil had let him think that for a long time. It had seemed easier than arguing over something that might never happen.

But now... He thought of leaving this farm, of crossing the cold sea, in a ship full of strangers, to a whole land of strangers. His heart turned to lead.

Slowly, heavily, he trudged up from the beach, past the fields and into the farmyard, and the house. He could see the red light of the kitchen fires shining through the partly open door, and he felt homesick, even though he hadn't left yet.

He went in, closing the door behind him, shutting out the dark. This, he thought, is a special time of day – the time when we shut out the night and cold; and we sit together, and eat, talk and laugh. It wouldn't be the same with strangers.

The kitchen was hot. Smoke hung in the air from

a few feet above the floor to the rafters, where it filtered out through the thatch. It had the throat-catching nip of burning peat.

Figures moved in the haze – busy women, getting together enough food to feed a large, tired, hungry household. There was a clang and clatter of iron pots and ladles.

A leather curtain hung to Ketil's right, dividing the kitchen from the living quarters. He pulled the curtain aside, making the smoke billow in the draught.

The hall was crowded. Not only Ketil's family – his grandfather, father, mother, sisters – but their slaves and their farm-servants too, were all gathered in here to eat.

This room was also gloomy with smoke, which coiled up from the central fire and hung in the air. Straw covered the floor, mixed with dried thyme, which released its scent when trodden on. The smell of peat mixed with that of the oil in the lamps, and the roasted meat and baked fish. It mixed with the smell of dogs, and sweaty people, and the grassy mustiness of the thatch... It was the smell of home.

Ketil edged among the people and dogs to reach his usual place on the benches, near the middle, near the fire. His grandfather sat there already, eating a bowl of porridge. He said, "Ketta! You've been out a long time! Good luck?"

Ketil remembered all the fish they'd caught, all eaten. "No luck," he said.

"I was getting worried," his mother said, and handed him a wooden plate holding flatbread, butter and cheese.

"Ottar's going to join a ship," he said. Everyone nearby who heard him stopped talking and looked at him. He wished he hadn't said it. "You know he's always talking about joining the Great Army. There's a ship at Lerwick..."

Ketil's father said, "More fool him."

"Aye," his grandfather agreed. "That sort are the worst sort of men."

"Why?" Ketil asked.

"Thieves and pirates – Vikings!" his father said. "If a ship full of that sort came here, killed me and your mother—"

"Thor keep us safe!" Ketil's mother said with a laugh as she handed Ketil a cup of ale.

"Well, you wouldn't like it," his father said. "Why think them heroes because the people they kill are Saxons? Vikings are rats and vipers."

Ketil half agreed, but at the same time was annoyed that his father always thought he knew best. "You're a rat and a viper, then." His parents and grandfather looked at him in surprise. "Ottar's mother says our people came from the sea and took this land," Ketil said. "She says you didn't work for it – you stole it."

"That was a long time ago," his father said. "Before your grandfather was born."

"Aye," Ketil's grandfather agreed. "My father took this land. There wasn't much killing from what I've heard."

"It was still stolen," Ketil said.

"Aye," said his grandfather, "but before I was born, so what could I do about it? I've never killed or stolen from anybody – nor has your father. And this farm'll come to you when we've gone – so you've got your land. You don't need to go killing Saxons."

"You're not to go! You can't go – tell him he can't go!"

Harald, Ottar's father, only turned his head away.

The hall at Ottar's home was smaller than the one at Ketil's, and even more crowded. Servants and slaves pretended to be thinking only of eating, while listening hard to the family's quarrel.

Ottar was making up the bundle of things he meant to take with him. His spears, axe and shield were propped against the wall, while he struggled to stuff his thick leather jerkin and cap into a sack.

"I'm going, mother," he said. "Whatever you say. So save some breath to cool your porridge."

"How can you talk to me like that?" she cried, her voice rising sharply. "Why are you so stupid? Can't you see that you'll only get killed and go to Hell? I say you can't go!"

The angrier and more desperate she became, the calmer Ottar felt. After he'd left Ketil, as he'd walked home, he'd been full of fears, both large and small. Here was his chance – but it was easy to dream about leaving home to fight battles and win gold. It was much harder to do it. Where would he sleep at night? What if he was cold and hungry? What if he made no friends and was all alone?

But he'd have Ketil.

What if Ketil wouldn't come? What if he really had to go, among all those grown men, on his own? Would he have the guts?

As he'd walked through the dark, he'd fretted

over these things until he felt queasy – but now, with his mother shrieking, it seemed simple. He couldn't stay here, with her shrilling at him like that. He wasn't a child any more.

"Mother," he said, "you can't tell me what to do because I'm a man. And I won't go to Hell because I'm not a Christian."

His father made a noise something like a laugh.

"Oh, it's funny, is it?" his wife shouted at him. "It's funny that your son's going off to be killed? He's too much like you!"

"Thank Thor he's like me!" said Harald. "Now shut your mouth, woman."

"I won't shut—" But she did, because Harald stood up and slapped her hard across the mouth. Then she went away to her bed-closet, with a couple of her Pictish women, and cried noisily.

It's good that I'm getting out of here, Ottar thought.

"At least she's singing another tune," his father said, as his mother's sobs continued. "Stupid woman. Not everybody who goes raiding gets killed."

"It's good you're going," said Young Harald, Ottar's eldest brother. His other brother, Gorm, was away visiting. "If the wind's blowing the other way, we won't be able to smell your feet from the Humber."

"It's the shock of your going so suddenly," his father said. "That's what upset her."

"I have to go now," Ottar said, "while I have the chance."

"I know," his father said. "She'll get used to it." There was a long silence between them, though around them talk went on, and Ottar's mother could still be heard crying.

"You'll be off at first light?" Harald asked.

"Before. I don't want the ship to be gone."

"Ketil's going with you?"

"Aye," Ottar said, though he wasn't sure that Ketil would.

"I'll walk down with you, see you off," said his father.

"No!" Ottar said. "I'll be going early – don't bother!" The last thing he wanted was his father holding his hand.

Ketil didn't sleep that night, and at first light he was in the farmyard, looking down over the fields towards the sea. He couldn't imagine what it would be like to wake in the morning and not see this land, nor what it would be like to go for days – a year or more – without seeing or speaking to the people he knew.

But all the same, a voice inside him said, *You're a coward if you don't go... People will call you an oath-breaker... If you don't go, everyone will* know *you're a coward...*

He tried to think as Ottar did. They would sail away on this great ship, and everyone would envy them... They would fight battles and have adventures... This part, in his mind, was a blur of words from poems and stories: *There was axe-play and arrow-music... They spread a feast before the wolf, they fed the crows... The wound-bees flew...* When he tried to think what it would really be like, he could only think of his practice-fights with Ottar, or of the embarrassing tussle with Hrolf.

But anyway, after the battles, they would come home...

Back here, to this place; and wouldn't he be glad to see it!

They'd come home with lots of gold, a chest of it. And gold rings on their arms, gold round their necks, on their fingers, in their ears! Gold brooches holding their cloaks, gold buckles to their belts. They'd be invited everywhere, to tell of their adventures; everyone would think them great men. All the girls would give them the eye, and everyone would want to marry their daughters to them. But they'd marry each other's sisters instead. He'd choose the one closest to Ottar in age, he thought. Gunnvor had very dark hair and big grey eyes.

Wouldn't it be worth missing home for a while, for all that?

Others were coming from the house now, slaves and free servants, on their way to the fields or the animal sheds. He wished a few a good day, and then someone shouted his name. It was Ottar, coming along the path with a pack on his back. Ketil's heart felt heavy. Now he would have to decide.

Ottar trudged up, panting a little from the weight of his pack. He said, "Ready?"

After a long pause, Ketil said, "Not yet."

"We don't want to miss the ship!"

Ketil thought, for the last time, about saying no. But it was too cowardly. "I'll get my stuff," he said, and drifted towards the hall.

Ottar started to follow him, but then said, "I'll get your war-gear," and turned towards the storehouses.

Ketil went through the busy kitchen, and into the hall, where women were rolling up the straw-filled mattresses, and his grandfather was drinking a mug of small ale. No one took any notice as Ketil opened a chest, took out his pack, and filled it with clothes. As he chose a knife and buckled it to his belt, he was still thinking about staying at home. But he could see how it would be without Ottar. There would be the farm, and his family, and the work – but in the long summer evenings, and the long winter nights, he would have no special friend. There would be no one to go visiting with, lending him courage to try and talk to girls; no one to go fishing with; no one to make a team with at harvest and haymaking, and compete against the others.

And anyway the ship would probably be gone when they reached Lerwick.

Shouldering his pack, he went out to the yard.

Ottar was waiting by the storehouse, with sacks holding Ketil's weapons and leather jerkin. It was an awkward load to carry, but Ketil managed to get it all in his arms or slung on his back. They started for the beach.

Ketil called to a couple of slaves, who were repairing the byre roof, and told them to come along, to help with the boat. He didn't say goodbye to anyone.

CHAPTER FOUR

An Oath

THE *WAVE STRIDER* WAS STILL in the bay at Lerwick. Ottar laughed aloud, seeing all his hopes for his life coming true. Ketil could only hope, miserably, that the shipmen would say they'd been joking, and send them home.

But the men welcomed them, helped them drag their boat up the beach, slapped them on the back, and shouted for Eyulf. He came sauntering from his tent, checked over their weapons and gear, and said they were "good enough". "If I take you into my war-band," he said, "you'll have to swear an oath to follow me, obey me and fight for me."

"Aye, I'll swear!" Ottar said, and his voice squeaked, which made the men laugh. Ottar laughed too, from nervousness.

Ketil didn't speak, but only shifted where he stood. Eyulf gave him a hard look. "And you?"

Ketil opened his mouth, but couldn't make himself say yes or no. He coughed and made a sidelong movement of his head that could have meant either.

"Come on, then," Bjorn said. "Let's have an oath-taking. You! Bring that chest over here."

A sea chest was waiting to be loaded onto the ship. A couple of men brought it over, and Eyulf sat on it. He unstrapped his sheathed sword, took it from its belt, and tucked it under his right arm with the hilt resting on his knee.

"Right," Bjorn said to Ottar. "Down on your knees in front of him."

Ottar went down on his knees in the shingle, with a sweet pain in his heart. This was so wonderful! He was taking an oath to his leader beside a great ship – just like a story! The chill wind shifted in his hair, the sea sighed on the shingle, gulls cried overhead; and tears came to Ottar's eyes.

Bjorn said quietly, "Start by telling us your family…"

Ottar knew, from stories, the sort of thing he should say. And a hero shouldn't mumble, so he called out, "I am Ottar Haraldssen, the son of Thorhart, the son of Thorstein, and I come from a mighty family—"

There was laughter, and someone called out, "A mighty family of sheep-chasers!"

The laughter stung Ottar, and made him flush. Ketil was embarrassed for him, and he expected Eyulf or Bjorn to call the men to order. But neither of them said anything, as if it was normal to be rude to guests and strangers.

"Now, put your right hand under Eyulf's," Bjorn said, and Ottar did. Eyulf's hand was clenched round the hilt of his sword, and felt hot. Bjorn muttered, "Say after me…"

Ottar's voice rang out clearly, repeating Bjorn's words: "I shall always heed the words of Eyulf, my leader. Never shall I refuse to do as he orders. I shall fight for Eyulf and the fellowship of Wave Strider: not one step shall I run from a battle. Always shall I deal fairly with Eyulf and my fellows, not keeping from them their due. If Eyulf or any of my fellows are killed, I shall avenge them. I, Ottar, make this oath, and never shall any need to reproach me for breaking it!"

"Now kiss the sword-hilt and his hand," Bjorn whispered.

Ottar did, and some of the men whooped and cheered. Ottar looked up with a big smile on his face, and tears on his cheeks. He looked up at Eyulf, because he knew that, now, Eyulf had to make his side of the vow.

Eyulf tossed his head high to throw wind-blown hair clear of his face. He said, "I am Eyulf Thorgeirssen, who was Olaf's son, who married the famous lady Astrid, daughter of Harald the Tall. All know I come of a famous, wealthy and respected family; and I am shipmaster of *Wave Strider* and leader of her war-band.

"I take this man, Ottar, as my man, and I shall reward him well for his service to me, with gifts and a share of all we win in battle. I shall feed him and guard him, and never be slow to speak up for him. If he is killed, I shall take vengeance for his death.

"No man who hears this shall ever have cause to rebuke me for not keeping my word!"

Eyulf stood, pulled Ottar to his feet and hugged

him before pulling a ring from his finger and giving it to him. Ottar looked at the ring and then at Ketil with a big, bright grin on his face, happier than Ketil had ever seen him.

Eyulf seated himself again, and tucked his sword back under his right arm. Bjorn pointed at Ketil. "Now you." He pointed at the ground in front of Eyulf.

Ketil stumbled forward, his face red and hot, his legs stiff and clumsy with embarrassment. He was trying over words in his head: *I don't need to take an oath because I'm not coming... I'm staying here...* He couldn't say them.

He kneeled at Eyulf's feet, because that was what everyone was waiting for him to do. He put his hand under Eyulf's right hand, under the sword-hilt, as he was told to do. All the time he was thinking: *I don't want to do this.*

"I am Ketil Arnassen, the son of Hart." He stopped. He couldn't think of anything to say about his family. They weren't famous, or wealthy.

Bjorn started to prompt him in a whisper, and he repeated the words, promising to obey Eyulf, to fight for him, to avenge him after his death, and to deal fairly with his fellows.

"I, Ketil, make this oath, and never shall any man have to reproach me for breaking it!" And he kissed Eyulf's sword-hilt and hand.

Eyulf made his reply, promising to reward Ketil and protect him. Then he stood, lifted Ketil up, hugged him, and gave him a ring from his finger.

Ketil stumbled back, his face full of dismay at what he'd sworn. The men cheered.

From the pouch at his belt, Bjorn took two oval slips of wood, and gave one each to the boys. The slips had the same shape burned on them, a shape that was a little like the curved prow of a ship meeting the curve of a wave. "This token means that you are now of the fellowship of Wave Strider. Show this token to any man here, and he will take you as his brother. Show it to men from any other ship, and they will help you."

Ottar took the little piece of wood as if it was more precious than the ring. Ketil looked at the wooden token, and thought: *Oh Father Thor, what have I let myself in for?*

"Get your gear stowed on board," Eyulf said. "Hrolf – show them where."

Both boys gathered up their gear and trudged across the beach after Hrolf. A boarding ladder was set against *Wave Strider*'s side, and Ottar ran up eagerly, not even getting his feet wet. Ketil passed up their things to him, and while he stood there, a wave rushed in further than the others and soaked his feet. *Wonderful*, he thought. *Now I have wet feet too.*

He climbed the ladder, went over the side, and was on the deck of the biggest ship he'd ever been aboard in his life. He could smell the pine and pitch of her decks, the leather of her walrus-hide ropes... Hrolf showed them how to stow their gear under the aft-deck.

Not long after, when all the packs and tents were aboard, they went back down to the beach, and put their shoulders to the ship, along with most of the rest of the crew. They strained, grunted and heaved together, and the ship moved grudgingly, then slid, then floated – and they had to scramble up the rope ladders again. Forty men took their places on the rowing benches, and Eyulf took his at the steering-oar. On the word of command, the men heaved at the oars – and the ship quivered and responded like a well-trained horse. She moved across the water, out into the bay, heading for the sea... Even Ketil couldn't help feeling thrilled. Ottar couldn't stop grinning.

* * *

Hours later, when the slaves had laboriously rowed back to Ketil's farm, Ketil's parents learned that their son had joined a ship bound for Northumbria and the Great Army.

"You must go and fetch him back!" Ketil's mother cried. "Hurry! If the wind's with you, you might reach them—"

"How can I do that?" Ketil's father asked. "He's a grown man."

"He might be a man in years, but he's still just a baby! Fetch him back!"

"If he's chosen to ignore our advice and take fellowship on a ship, it's not for me to tell him anything. Let him learn the hard way."

Ketil's mother started to sob. "He'll be killed – he'll be ill – you could fetch him back—"

"Hundreds sail away, and come back as healthy as they left," her husband said. "They also come back as poor and as stupid as they left, but they come back. So hold your noise, woman, and give us some peace."

Chapter Five

The Fort

THE *WAVE STRIDER* SAILED for a day and night, while the boys learned how the wind and salt-spray could scrape their faces sore, and how hard a ship's boards were to sleep on. When the sea emerged from darkness again, dancing in sun-dazzle, they glimpsed Orkney's great rock stack in the distance, and the mountains of Northern Pictland came into view. They kept on another day and another night, and then they were in view of the Pictish coast.

They beached the ship in a bay, and spent a night ashore, with fires and hot food; and, next morning, pushed off again. For three more days they travelled, beaching at night, and on the fourth day came into the wide mouth of the river Tyne, in Northumbria, where Halfdan had made his winter quarters.

A cold wind blew across the wide estuary, and gulls screamed all around them. On the muddy shore were huddles of huts – rough things of driftwood and turf, with boats drawn up near them, and drying frames for fish, and spread nets. Fishing villages – but there was no smoke, and no sign of people.

The river narrowed, and they rowed through fenland clamouring with birds. Good country, Ketil thought, looking round. Fish, geese, duck... There'd be eels too. And beaver. You could keep a family on what you could catch by this river! No wonder the Army came here.

Ottar and Ketil had wandered forward, near the prow. "There!" said a man, breathlessly, as he rowed, and looked awkwardly over his shoulder, with a nod. They looked in that direction and saw, rearing up over the riverbanks, a hill of raw, dirty earth, and a timber wall above. In the sky hung a smudge of smoke. That was the fort, Halfdan's winter quarters, the place where they would join the Great Army. From that direction came a clatter of noise, both carried and muffled by the wind – a gabble of shouts, hammering, dogs barking... There was a tang of peat-smoke in the air.

Ketil felt a dart of panic go through him, and his heart beat faster. They'd arrived. This was where he would fight battles... He felt his flesh shrink on his bones, as if trying to creep away from the heavy, sharp blades that would strike at it. He looked at Ottar, and Ottar was grinning as if on his way to a feast. *He must be braver than me*, Ketil thought.

As they rounded more bends, the fort loomed. They came to a place where another, smaller river joined the Tyne, and made a wide pool. Here scores of ships swayed at anchor, some with their masts up, others with them shipped, all with their sails furled. The hulls were painted red and black, blue and yellow, and gilding gleamed on bows and figureheads.

They were right under the fort now, and the clamour of people was louder, the smell of smoke and cesspits stronger.

A small war-boat, long and sleek, shot out from among the ships, coming to meet them. Armed men, several with bows, stood on the deck. One man bawled at them, "Who are you?"

Eyulf gave the steering-oar to Bjorn and bounded forward to lean over the bulwarks and speak to the armed men. They shouted back and forth at each other, but it was hard to hear anything they said.

Wave Strider's men were quieter than usual, waiting, using their oars to keep *Wave Strider* steady, and to fend her off the tethered boats. It was oddly peaceful, as they waited, despite the fort, and the armed men. There was the sound of the water passing them, and dripping off the oars; the wind in the ropes, the calling of geese and ducks – and, more distantly, the shouting from the fort, and the striking of iron on iron.

Eyulf straightened, shouting orders, and the smaller ship shot past them. The men took up oars again, Eyulf went back to the steering-oar, and *Wave Strider* was carefully steered among the other ships, and anchored. There she swayed, in a town of ships.

Ketil and Ottar looked about from her deck. There were other fast, sleek warships, some bigger and more richly decorated, but with the same long, lean shape. Others were broader and heavier, with fewer oars but thicker masts and bigger sails – cargo ships, here to supply the Army.

Beyond the ships was the riverbank, with wooden piers and jetties, and long, low sheds of timber and turf. Men jostled among stacks of barrels, rope and timbers.

Further back, beyond the piers, were more buildings, and more people; there was smoke from fires, and a clamour of yelling, of dogs barking, pigs squealing, chickens chattering, of carts, of hammering – all the noise of a busy, crowded town.

Neither Ketil nor Ottar had ever seen so many people, animals and buildings in one place before, nor heard so much noise. In Shetland, not even the biggest town was as big as this frightening place.

Eyulf yelled, "I'm going ashore! Bjorn, you're in charge."

Eyulf was rowed away between the taller ships in *Strider*'s little boat. Ketil and Ottar wished they could go too, just to set foot on shore, but Bjorn came along and put them to work. He wanted everything that they would need to take ashore – the tents, cooking gear, food, and each man's weapons and belongings – stacked ready in tidy piles.

When Eyulf returned, they loaded everything

into the boats, ferried it all ashore, and humped it through the crowds on the riverbank, and up the hill to the place where Eyulf said they were to camp. They came closer to the stronghold, and saw that there was a deep, water-filled ditch all round it. The earth dug from the ditch had been thrown up into a high, steep bank, hard-trodden. The wall of pitch-painted timber above it had a gate, and armed men could be seen on top of the gate and walls.

Crews of various ships were camped all round the stronghold. Some were living in tents, others had built themselves shacks of turf and timber, some roofed with upturned boats. They were greeted as they trudged by.

"West Fjord men?"

"Shetland!" Ottar called out, jerking his thumb at himself and Ketil.

"Aah! Shetlanders are sheep!" But some of the men already camped came and helped them set up their tents and build fires. By the time that was done, it was dusk.

"Are you away up to the hall the night?" one of their new friends asked. He was a big redhead from a ship called *Sea Worm*.

Ottar elbowed Ketil and giggled with excitement.

He was dizzy with the knowledge that he was here, as he'd always dreamed, with Halfdan's Army, in Northumbria, and about to feast with Halfdan, like a hero. He was disappointed in Ketil, who pulled a long face.

Their new, red-headed friend talked as the whole crew walked up to the stronghold. "Winter quarters, this. We've been fighting all year – here in the north, and all through Mercia. Whoo! We've seen some fighting. The Saxons round here thought they'd get their own back, see, and we had to put 'em right about that. Halfdan's storehouses are full anyway – he'll be filling our ship with gold when we leave – he'd better! We fought hard enough for him!"

"You've fought Saxons?" Ottar said. "What are they like?"

The redhead laughed aloud. "I tell you, when Halfdan came here, he walked into York without so much fight as you'd get from a kitchen girl! Not so much as a slap and a squeal! They were having one of their Christian holidays. Much too busy with that to fight!"

The men of the *Wave Strider* laughed in disbelief.

"It's true! Walked in without a fight! Plenty of

'Oh Christ save us!' but no courage!"

The men laughed again. "We're going to be rich, then!" Eyulf said.

"Oh, we're all going to be rich! And you'll eat well tonight! The Saxons couldn't decide which one of 'em to make king, so Halfdan's decided for 'em! And Halfdan's little tame Saxon king eats out of Halfdan's hand and does everything Halfdan tells him! 'What's that, Halfdan?' little kingy says. 'You want fifty wagons of grain delivered to your stronghold, and a hundred cattle and a hundred sheep? I'll see to it right away, Halfdan!' The Saxons starve, but we eat well!"

Ketil, falling behind the rest, thought it was just as his father and grandfather had said: the Army was robbing the Saxon farmers. True, they were only Saxons – but they were also farmers, like his own family.

But he was here – he was one of those robbing bullies. He was going to eat food stolen from Saxon farms.

They walked under the high earthen bank of the stronghold, and could smell the soil, and the rank water of the ditch. They crossed the ditch by a wooden bridge that could easily be chopped down, if the stronghold came under attack; and entered through the gate, which smelled of wood and pitch. Men armed with spears were on guard, and watched them pass.

Many buildings were crammed inside the stronghold's walls. Kitchens. A God-house for Thor, Odin and Frey. Guarded storerooms, barracks, stables and byres, pigsties, henhouses and smithies. They threaded through these low buildings – some of them little more than roofed holes in the ground.

At the centre of it all was Halfdan's hall. Ketil thought it a poor place, thrown up hurriedly from whatever was at hand – turfs, old ship's timbers, new, ill-weathered timber, even oiled cloth, weighted down. It wasn't as well-built as the farmhouse at home.

Ottar was disappointed for an eye-blink – but then thought: *This is Halfdan's hall!* Halfdan Ragnarsson son of Ragnar Lothbrok, the sea-lord, and leader of the Great Army! This was the rough-hewn lair of a pirate-king. And when Halfdan was truly king of this land, he would replace this hall with a finer one – and reward the men who had helped him. And he, Ottar, would be one of them.

The doors of the hall stood open, letting out firelight and a welcoming smell of roast meat. Inside, the light of the torches glared through a haze of smoke, which started them all coughing.

Long benches ran the length of the hall and somewhere at the head of it, hidden in firelit smoke, was the table where Halfdan sat. Ottar hoped they would see him. Even Ketil was curious.

The crew of the *Strider* claimed places on a bench. Women scurried about, bringing ale and bread – they looked scared, and one had a bruised face. Their speech sounded Saxon, and Ketil guessed that the women were enslaved Saxon prisoners. How would he feel if it was his sisters, looking cowed like that?

A man came through the smoke, calling Eyulf's name. Eyulf stood, and the man said, "Come now, and make your vows to Halfdan."

Every man of the *Wave Strider* clambered from behind the table, and followed Eyulf down the hall past the long, crowded, noisy tables. They wanted to see him make his vows, because when he promised to serve Halfdan, he would be binding all of them to Halfdan's service; and the reward Halfdan promised him would be their reward too.

The high table appeared through the smoke. Halfdan's hall might be a mere pirate-king's lair, but his table was raised a good step above the rest of the hall, to make it clear that he *was* the king. The man who had fetched them stepped onto the platform and spoke to a balding man seated at the table's centre. The man rose and came round the table, stepped down from the platform. "You are Eyulf Thorgeirssen?" He almost shouted – a man used to bellowing across fields, and unused to lowering his voice.

Ottar realized that this was the great Halfdan Ragnarsson. He'd imagined Halfdan as tall, young and handsome, dressed in coloured clothes and decked in gold.

In fact, Halfdan was old. He was tall, and he wore a red shirt, and blue and white striped trews – but he had a paunch, his face was leathery and wrinkled and his beard and scanty hair were grey.

"You wish to serve me?" Halfdan demanded in his loud voice that carried down the hall.

"For reward," Eyulf said, and his men laughed. That was their Eyulf, ever ready to speak up for himself – and them.

Halfdan smiled. "For reward, aye, for reward – I

don't think a man risks his life for me for nothing. There'll be reward enough for you and all your crew – the Saxons are rich!"

A servant brought a stool to Halfdan, and another brought his sword. Halfdan sat on the stool and tucked his sword under his right arm, just as Eyulf had done.

Eyulf didn't need to be told what to do. He went down on both knees, and shouted out his name, and his father's and grandfather's, and what a powerful and wealthy family he came from.

Then he put his hand under Halfdan's sword-hilt, and said, "I have fought in Ireland, and in Frankland; and I have killed many. I have won gold, and given it away; and I shall fight for Halfdan. I shall kill many of his enemies, and the gold that Halfdan gives me, I shall give away."

Ottar, grinning with excitement, nudged Ketil.

"I swear that I shall always fight before Halfdan, will defend him, and avenge him if need be. I shall fight to the death rather than take one step to leave the battlefield. And never shall I forget the gifts I shall get from Halfdan; never shall I forget to praise him."

Ottar was hugging himself with glee.

Eyulf said, "No man who hears me swear this oath shall ever need to say that I did not keep my words." And he kissed Halfdan's hand and sword-hilt.

A roar broke out that made Ketil flinch. The "Striders" were clapping, stamping, whistling – people at the table were pounding their fists and knives on the board. Striders were celebrating their tie to Halfdan, and the rewards to come. Everyone else was welcoming a new troop to the Army.

Halfdan held up his free hand and silence fell as he made his part of the vow. He promised to make battles for them, and to lead in the fight; to reward their service; and to protect and guard them.

He then raised Eyulf up and embraced him – deafening noise broke out again – and gave him an armband, before returning to his seat at the high table.

A man darted from the smoke with a bundle of tally sticks in his hand, and said to Eyulf, "How long will your service be?"

"Two years," Eyulf said.

Two years! Ketil thought. It was for ever. And never to see home in all that time.

Two years!

CHAPTER SIX
Chores

WHEN *WAVE STRIDER* REACHED the fort, it was still early in Leaf-Fall Season. The mornings were chilly, the nights cold, and the days growing shorter, but real cold was still to come. Before winter, both the fort and their fellowship house had to be finished.

So Eyulf and Bjorn roused everybody from their beds before light, with shouts and kicks. If they still slept, they pulled down their tent. Many of the men had drunk too much, and their heads throbbed as they crawled out of their tent's wreckage.

"What do I care if your head aches?" Eyulf said.

"I'm not your mammy!"

On the first day, Ketil and Ottar were sent up to the fort. Ottar had some idea that they were being sent to Halfdan, who would lead them out to fight Saxons. He was disappointed to be ordered – and not by Halfdan either – to dig a ditch. Together with many other men, and some slaves, they were to enlarge the ditch that ran between the two rivers, defending the fort from the landward side. It had to be made wider and deeper, while the earth dug from it was thrown up onto the bank, to make it steeper and harder to climb. The loose earth had to be pounded and stamped down, to compact it.

Ketil was relieved. He'd dug ditches before, on the farm.

But this was harder work than any field-ditch. Back in Shetland, Ketil and Ottar had heard of forts being built, of "ditches being dug and banks being raised". It was quick and easy to say. They'd imagined it done between one eye-blink and another.

What's easy to tell is hard to do. Bending their backs to every shovelful, and straightening their backs against the weight of every wet, heavy load of earth, was hard, hard work. It rained, and their clothes stuck to them, heavy and clammy. The wet wool scraped their skin whenever they moved. They slipped and fell bruisingly, and became plastered in mud from their hair to their feet, so they weighed heavier and heavier as the day went on. Sometimes they could hardly lift their feet for the weight of mud stuck to them.

"Why are we doing slaves' work?" Ottar said. "Digging ditches isn't work for warriors! We should be fighting! Getting gold!"

One of the men beside them – a mud man – laughed. "Is the work too hard for you, girls? Did you think it was going to be all fighting and feasting? That's only in Valhalla – and I hope it's going to be a long time before I see that place!"

Another man, leaning on his muddy knees and breathing hard, explained that there weren't enough slaves to do the work before winter, and if they wanted a fort to keep them and their ships safe from the Saxons, then they had to do the heavy work themselves.

Ottar decided to stop complaining then. If other warriors could dig ditches, then so could he... So long as he got to fight and win gold in the end.

The boys were tired out that night and, the next

morning, every little movement hurt, their muscles ached so much – but if they'd complained, they'd have been laughed at, and called girls or slaves. So they went to another day's work, despite their sore backs, sore arms, sore legs, sore hands...

Sometimes they were told to stay behind and work on the fellowship house, which was being built in a patch of ground crammed between other such houses. They built it in the simplest way – by digging a hole in the ground and roofing it. But the hole had to be dug, and it had to be deep, and stones had to be quarried out, and set aside, in case they might be useful later. It was all hard work.

Materials had to be gathered – turf for the low walls, timber for roof supports, heather to thatch the roof. It was no use looking for these materials nearby. The turf had already been stripped from the fort's hillside, to build other huts. The fort was a place of mud and raw earth. They had to leave the fort and walk a couple of miles before they could cut turf or heather, and load it onto a borrowed donkey. All timber of any size had already been cut down, even at that distance.

There was so little timber to be had that Eyulf had to buy some from a ship that had put in, paying with ounces of gold and silver. He had to break up one of his armbands to make the weight, and he wasn't happy about it.

While working the men were warm enough, but when they stopped, the wet mud and sweat plastered to them leached away their body heat, until they were chilled and shivering. There were fires, at their camp, but even as they warmed themselves, they were wondering how much fuel was left, and where they were going to get more. It quickly burned away to ash. There was never enough, and at the beginning and end of each day's work, it was the boys who were expected to go and find something to burn.

"It's women's work," Hakon said. "And work for slave-women at that – so, Ketil, Ottar – jump to it!"

This was a huge joke – and all the other men joined in, throwing small stones and bones at them, insisting that the boys go.

"Why is it always us?" Ketil asked. "It isn't fair."

But the men didn't care whether it was fair or not.

"Go and find fuel," Eyulf said. "That's an order."

Ottar and Ketil dragged on their cold, still damp clothes, which were filthy and stiff with mud, and chafed at every step. They ducked out of their stinking tent, which was at least warm, and trudged off through the waking camp, to find, or beg, or steal something which would burn.

It got harder all the time. They had to burn dried dung, or peat, or even cakes of pond scum. But this had to be dried for a year or even more before it would burn well, and although the fort was building up a stock of dried fuel for the years ahead, they had none ready to burn.

So it had to be taken from the Saxons. Halfdan's patrols went out every day, "commandeering" – or stealing – the Saxons' fuel. Most of it went on the fires in Halfdan's hall and kitchens. Some was given out to the men of the Army, but you had to be there earlier and earlier to get your share, and be prepared to push and shove, and then hurry away before it was taken from you.

If the boys succeeded, they slogged back through the mud to find the other Strider men still in bed, or helping themselves to whatever food was left for breakfast. The food had been collected from Halfdan's storehouses the night before – usually by Ketil and Ottar. There might be some flatbread and cheese left, if they were lucky.

Why am I here? Ketil wondered. *I hate it. I've never worked so hard in my life. I've never felt so tired, cold and hungry. I've never been so wet and dirty. Why, in the name of all the Gods did I come?*

It was his own fault, he knew. But a small part of him blamed Ottar. He tried not to. He had a tongue in his head: he could have said, "No, I'm staying at home." But the feeling kept sneaking back. It was all Ottar's fault.

Before the *Wave Strider* crew had finished eating, Halfdan's officers came round, harrying them to work – and it was back to the heavy labour and the mud. At the end of every day they were exhausted and hungry, but couldn't go to Halfdan's hall to eat while covered in filth. So they went back to their camp, where they pulled off all their clothes, and, shivering, washed off the worst of the mud with river water. And who had to carry the heavy wooden buckets down to the river, and lug them back uphill, filled with water and even heavier?

On reaching their shack, the *Strider* men threw themselves down on the ground. "Off you go," they said to Ketil and Ottar. "Hurry up."

When the boys brought back the water, the buckets were quickly surrounded by men, who stripped off and sloshed cups of water about. When the boys could reach the buckets, they were empty, and they had to go down to the river again.

"It isn't fair!" Ketil said.

Hakon set his fist against Ketil's ear, jokingly pushing his head to one side. "Life isn't fair! The Gods aren't fair! Get used to it!"

Eyulf was nearby, sitting on his sea chest. He'd changed his muddy work-clothes for cleaner ones, and was pulling on his still muddy boots. "Eyulf," Ketil called out. "We always fetch food in the morning and water at night – it's not fair. We work hard all day like everybody else. Somebody else should go sometimes."

Ottar nudged Ketil's shoulder, and whispered, "Don't go on about it!"

Eyulf said, "Your legs are the youngest."

"You're not old men!" Ketil looked round at them, as they pulled on boots or clean shirts, or tied coloured headbands about their brows. "Or are you – all old men?"

"I'm old and broken-down, me," said Hakon, who was perhaps twenty-five. "I can't hobble down to the river, Eyulf!"

"It's not *fair*!" Ketil said.

Eyulf stood, abruptly, angrily. "If you don't want to do it, don't do it! But don't bother me!"

Ketil and Ottar went down to the river together, to wash in the cold water. The men laughed at them as they went.

"We shouldn't do it," Ketil said.

Ottar said nothing. He was thinking that they'd be in a hard place if they fell out with the Strider men.

Ketil said, "If we keep doing all the work, they'll keep on letting us. We should say we're not doing it, like Eyulf told us."

"We're part of a ship's crew," Ottar said. "We have to obey orders."

"Who ordered us to do all the work?" Ketil demanded. "Eyulf didn't. Bjorn didn't. It's the others, being idle. And Eyulf *said* not to do it if we didn't think it fair."

Ottar grimaced, seeming half-convinced.

"They can't make us, if we stick together," Ketil said. "Like blood brothers." He knew Ottar would like that. "We'll stand together, like blood brothers. We'll say no, somebody else has to take a turn. Agreed?"

Ottar grinned. Maybe Ketil was right. If they stuck up for each other, maybe the men would listen.

"Agreed," he said, and they clasped hands. It felt almost as if they were winning battles already.

So, next morning, when they woke, and one of the men told them to fetch the food, Ketil said, "No."

A boot hit him on the hip.

"I'm not going," Ketil said.

"Neither am I!" said Ottar.

"It's somebody else's turn," Ketil said.

Other things were thrown at them – wooden cups, more boots, bones – but they stayed wrapped in their blankets. No one got up to fetch the food.

When Halfdan's captains came round, they had to get up, and put on their stiff, damp work clothes. There was still no food. Eyulf asked where it was.

"Ottar and Ketil didn't fetch it," someone said.

Eyulf said, "Go and get the food."

"No," Ketil said.

Eyulf looked at him, surprised. His eyes seemed very blue.

"You said, last night, that we shouldn't do it if it wasn't fair," Ketil said. "So we're not going. Send somebody else."

A shadow shifted before his eyes; there was a

great jolt at his head, another at his back, and he was looking at the sky.

Something struck him painfully in the side, and he rolled over. "Go get the food," Eyulf said, looking down at him.

All the Strider men were still and silent.

Ottar got hold of Ketil's arms and heaved him into a sitting position, then hauled him to his feet. Ketil staggered, putting his hand to his face, which throbbed. His hand came away with blood on it.

They set off for the stronghold in the chill half-dark. "He punched me!" Ketil said. He felt at his aching ribs. "And kicked me!"

Ottar nodded. His heart was beating faster, his thoughts in a flurry. He should have hit Eyulf – he knew he should – but how could he hit the shipmaster? He felt cowardly, and angry with himself, but you just didn't hit the shipmaster. None of the other men had said anything about Eyulf punching Ketil. They'd stood and watched.

It was as he'd feared – Ketil's moaning was turning all the men against them, getting them a reputation for being troublesome and disobeying orders. Ottar could see a day when he tried to take service with, say, Halfdan – and Halfdan said, "Oh, I remember you... You're the man who wouldn't obey his shipmaster." Ottar could see all his ambitions coming to nothing because Ketil didn't understand that, in a ship's crew, you had to do as you were told – especially if you were the newest and youngest member.

At the storehouses they were given the usual strings of dried fish, but the only bread left was the burned stuff that no one else wanted. When they returned with it, the men were angry, and took all the fish, and the best of the bread.

"It's your fault we got charcoal, so *you* eat it."

Ketil and Ottar were working on the fort's ditch that day, and they walked well behind the others. They didn't speak to each other. Ketil's face and ribs hurt, and he longed for home. It was all Ottar's fault, he felt, that he wasn't at home, listening to stories round the fireside.

Ottar, trudging beside him, felt angry and scared, because all the Strider men were angry with them, and it was Ketil's fault.

They didn't speak much to each other that day.

That evening they trudged back to the hut, caked in mud.

"Fetch the water," Hakon said, grinning.

Ketil drew breath, wondering whether he dared to argue.

Ottar said, "Aye, Ketil, off you go! Fetch water, serving-maid, and quick about it!"

The men laughed aloud. Hakon put his hand on Ottar's shoulder, and doubled over with laughter.

Ketil stood with his mouth open, shocked, which made the men laugh even more.

Hakon made shooing motions at him. "Go on! Get the water, girlie."

Ketil couldn't see what else he could do, unless he was going to fight the whole crew. Angry and miserable, he picked up the buckets and started for the river. Behind him, the men laughed.

Eyulf was pulling off his filthy shirt. He said to Ottar, "Go and help him."

Ottar didn't even think about answering back. He picked up another couple of buckets and followed Ketil.

There was a place at the river where the men had cut away the bank, so you could get close to the water, and dip a bucket easily. Ottar stood behind Ketil and waited, while Ketil filled his buckets.

Ottar said to Ketil's back, "It was only a joke."

Ketil heaved one full bucket aside, and dipped the second.

"You can't keep complaining," Ottar said. "We're with the Great Army! We have to be tough. Act the fool a bit – they'll like you for it."

As Ketil heaved up the second bucket, he gave Ottar a look as filthy as his clothes. He hefted his buckets, and walked away in silence.

That night, in Halfdan's hall, they sat apart. Ketil was beside Bjorn, but might as well have been alone. He looked at his food or stared at nothing. Ottar, his blood brother, was five places away, laughing with Hakon.

Chapter Seven
Thorkel "Do-It"

BY THE TIME THE COLD began to bite – when the mud, in the morning, was frozen hard – the fellowship house was finished. From the outside, it looked like a peaked roof of heather-thatch lying on the ground. The entrance was midway along one side, with steps roughly made of earth and stone leading down into thick, smoky darkness.

Inside, the only light came from the fire in its pit, or filtered in at the door. There were no windows. Platforms of hard-packed earth ran down either side, on which the men sat and slept. Eyulf's precious timbers propped up the roof, each one resting on a pad-stone to keep it from rotting. The house smelled of earth, and bruised grass and heather, and of thick smoke. It reeked of men – their stale breath, their sweaty armpits and sweat-soaked clothes, their sweaty feet. But it was warm, and it was mostly dry. After a hard day's work, it was luxury to lie down on one of the earthen benches, and wrap yourself in your cloak and blanket. It was the only place where the boys could lie down, feeling full after the meal in the hall, and be warm, even to the tips of their toes, fingers and ears; and sleep. No one shouted at them for the whole night.

Night in the fellowship house was the only time Ketil found bearable. All the time he was awake, his "fellows" were jeering at him. They hid his things, stole his food, tripped him up. They played jokes on Ottar too, but not nearly as often; and Ottar would laugh, and pretend he thought it all fun.

Ketil wouldn't ask Ottar to stick up for him, because that would be shaming, but he thought that Ottar ought to help him. Ottar didn't. Eyulf didn't either, and it was surely Eyulf's job to look after his men.

Ketil wanted to ask Ottar if he missed home and regretted joining Wave Strider too, but he didn't ask, in case Ottar accused him of whining again. They didn't talk much any more, anyway.

One thing was better: they no longer fetched the water, firewood, or food, because the Strider men had bought some slave-women from other crews. There was an older woman, with greying hair, and two girls. They were Saxons, and pathetic creatures, all of them. The men never left any of them alone. Their lives were miserable, but they didn't run away because they had nowhere to go. Their own families, even if they were still alive, wouldn't take them back. The women scuttled about, trying to make themselves small with lowered heads and hunched shoulders. Ketil once reached for his cup while the older woman was near him, and she cowered, expecting a blow. It made him feel sad.

Ketil ducked out of the house. He often walked about the camp by himself, to get away from the men he had shipped with. He tried to interest himself in the ships, or the animal pens, or any work being done, so he wouldn't have to think of home. If he started picturing what his family would be doing now, then he saw them all, in his mind, so clearly that it hurt.

He saw some men on the practice-grounds, so he headed over there, and was pleased to find that they were Bison men, practising archery. He'd come to know some of them a little, and stopped to watch.

A voice behind him said, "Glum again?"

Ketil felt cheered as he turned. He was miserable in this place, but there were a few people who weren't so bad. Red Grim was one of them.

Red Grim was grinning through his short ginger beard. His skin was very brown, and wrinkled around his mouth and across his forehead, though he wasn't so old. His eyes were very light against his darkened skin. "Put your backs into it!" he suddenly yelled at the archers, steam spurting from his mouth. "Let's see you get within a boat's length of the target – that'd make a change!" Looking at Ketil, he said, "Any good with a bow?"

"Not much."

"Let's see." Grim fetched a bow that was leaning against some quivers.

Ketil took it, feeling all his muscles tighten, and his arms and fingers become awkward, because he was being watched. The bow was already strung.

"Let me see how you draw up," Grim said.

Ketil tried, but it was a powerful bow. He couldn't draw it. Grim quickly took it from him and handed him another, then stood aside and watched as Ketil drew up. He held the bow at full draw for a second before letting it down. He didn't loose the string, because he knew that, if he did, the power that would have sent an arrow flying would run through him instead, rattling his teeth, rattling every joint.

"Keep that one," Grim said, and fetched him a quiver of arrows. "See how close you can get to the target."

The target was a cow's skull on the ground. The men weren't trying to hit it, but to drop their arrows near it. In battle, they wouldn't be trying to hit any one man, but to let a frightening, confusing, wounding shower of arrows fall in the same spot, at the same range.

Ketil nocked an arrow to his string, feeling that his arms and fingers were all too long and too thick. He wanted to impress Grim, but felt sure he was going to make a fool of himself again.

He did. He couldn't have done it if he'd been trying. He didn't know how he did it. Somehow, he shot the bow forward an arm's length, while the arrow dropped at his feet.

Some men nearby laughed. Red-faced, and trying to fold his tall body up small, Ketil took a quick look at Grim.

Grim said, "Go and walk round, till you've walked some sense back."

So Ketil walked round the camp – down to the muddy shore and ships, between the fellowship houses of turf and timber, almost up to the ditch surrounding Halfdan's hall – talking to himself all the time. "It's only shooting! You've done it scores of times."

When he went back, the bow was where he'd left it. He took it up, nocked an arrow to the string, drew up, loosed, nocked another arrow, loosed, nocked an arrow, drew up – and the first arrow hit the ground a foot's length from the cow's skull.

The second arrow hit the ground a hand's span beyond the skull, and the third landed so close to the second that the shafts knocked together.

A couple of Bison's men cheered. Grim raised his brows, and said, "Not half bad. Could be faster, but good style."

Ketil felt his face shift into a big grin. He felt

happier, for that moment, than since he'd joined Wave Strider.

"Remember to keep your bow arm solid," Grim said. "Don't let your wrist bend at all."

Ketil shot again. A couple of other archers came over and watched him carefully, making him nervous, but not as much as before.

"You're plucking the string when you loose," one man said. "Never do that."

"Just straighten your fingers to let the string go," said the other. "Never pluck it."

"Ah, you can spend your whole life learning to loose the string," said Grim, and the other two nodded.

Ketil felt he was in another world with these men, who didn't jeer or boast or squabble, but talked quietly about skill and practice. He spent the rest of the day there, learning, practising and improving. When the Bison men went back to their fellowship house, he went with them.

Their house was just as crowded and dark and reeking with smoke and stinks as the Strider house. The men shouted, some of them were drunk – and yet, it was different. They had slave-women; and they weren't *kind* to them, but they didn't torment them either. They bickered and taunted each other, but when one man stood, seeming about to lose his temper, a voice roared through the smoke. The man looked startled, and sat down.

"The shipmaster," Grim said, explaining the loud voice. "Thorkel Do-It."

The man on Ketil's other side said, "That's what he always shouts – '*Do it!*' If anybody's slow, if anybody argues – 'Do it!'"

"Nobody argues with him," Grim said.

"His wife does!" the other man said.

Grim grinned. "Oh, *she* does – and his daughters give him grief. But *we* don't dare argue!"

"We just *do it*!" said the other man, and there was a big laugh. Even one of the slave-women joined in, and no one hit her for impertinence.

Sitting there, in the crush, the heat and the smoke, Ketil thought: *If I have to be here at all, I should be with the Bison men.*

He said, "Can I join you?"

Grim and the other men looked at him blankly.

"I want to join Bison."

Now the men looked uneasy. "Why would you want to do that?" Grim asked.

"I don't like Wave Strider."

"Didn't you take a vow to Wave Strider?" asked the man on Ketil's other side.

"Aye, and I kept my vow," Ketil said. "Eyulf made a vow to me as well, and he hasn't kept his. I'm picked on all the time. I don't like serving with him. I want a better leader."

Grim and the other men looked at each other. "You could tell your leader you're leaving him, and give him his token back – but are you sure you want to do that?"

"It'll cause ill-feeling," the other man said.

"I'm sure," Ketil said.

"Think it over," Grim said. "Don't rush into a thing like that."

"I've made up my mind," Ketil said.

"Then ask our Thorkel if he'll have you," Grim said.

That was a frightening thought – but as soon as he felt scared, Ketil decided that he would do it anyway. He was only here because he'd been too scared to say no to joining the Army. He wasn't going to let being scared stop him again. "I'll ask him now." He stood.

Grim put a hand on his arm. "Best wait until we've been up to the hall. Then he'll have eaten, have some drink in him – he'll be in a better mood."

So, that night, Ketil ate in the hall with the Bison men. He saw the Strider crew looking at him curiously, but ignored them. And after the meal, he went back to the Bison house.

Thorkel Do-It was standing outside with his hands tucked into his armpits, his thumbs sticking up. He was looking at the sky, judging the weather. Ketil, with Grim at his shoulder, went up to him, and said, "Shipmaster, may I speak with you?" He sounded bold, even to his own ears. Inside, he quaked.

It was hard to see Thorkel Do-It in the dark, but he'd seen him clearly enough in the firelit hall. Thorkel was a big man, with a big square head, and a square face weathered brown and red. Sandy-fair hair fell over his deeply wrinkled brow.

Thorkel gave an unexpectedly friendly grin. "Speak up!"

Ketil's mouth went dry, and he couldn't speak. Grim nudged him. "You were lippy enough just now – spit it out!"

"Aye, do it!" Thorkel said.

Ketil felt like laughing at that, but managed to say, "I want to join Bison, and make my oaths to you."

Thorkel gave several quick nods, looking from Ketil to Grim. He said, "You must already be in a fellowship."

"I'm with Wave Strider."

Thorkel stared at him. "You can't be in two fellowships."

"I know. I'm going to give Eyulf his token back."

There was a silence. They could hear the river running through the dark below them, and the sighing and creaking of the ships at anchor.

Ketil felt, from the silence, that leaving Wave Strider was harder than he'd ever thought it would be. He said, hurriedly, "I know I promised to serve Eyulf, and I have, but – they pick on me and shove me around, and I hate it!"

Thorkel leaned towards Ketil and said, "Run back to mammy! Why would I want such a big baby in my crew?"

Ketil's face turned hot, and there were tears in his eyes. He would have given up and slunk off, but Grim poked him in the back. Ketil took that to mean he should stand up for himself, so he said, "I'm not a baby! I served Eyulf as best I could – and he made a vow too! He vowed to protect me, and he didn't! He hit me and knocked me down because I wouldn't do all the chores all the time! I'll do my fair share, but I'm a free man, not a slave – why should I always do the worst chores? And all of them pick on me, and steal my things, and trip me up – and Eyulf says and does nothing. He can't keep order in his crew. Why should I stand for it?"

Thorkel nodded several times, looked at Grim, and coughed.

No one said anything in words, but Ketil realized that Eyulf wasn't a good leader, and that Thorkel and Grim knew he wasn't, though they would never say so.

Thorkel said, "Listen, son. Giving your oath to a man is a serious thing. You can't break it because he doesn't kiss you goodnight like your mammy did. Did you expect life to be as easy in the Army as it was on the farm?"

Ketil found his head hanging down even though he tried to hold it up. "No," he muttered.

"Why complain, then? Go back and lump it. You chose to take an oath to Eyulf – you must have known what he was like."

Ketil's head still hung. He didn't feel like admitting that he'd taken an oath to Eyulf when he hadn't known him at all. He felt a fool.

"It would cause bad feeling between Strider and Bison," Thorkel said. "Halfdan wouldn't like it. *I* wouldn't like it. So, no."

Without looking at Thorkel or Grim, Ketil turned and ran away, back to his own fellowship house.

CHAPTER EIGHT
Winter Quarrel

NEXT MORNING, KETIL WAS SITTING in the near-dark of the fellowship house, eating a dried fish, when Eyulf sat opposite him and said, "I hear you've been creeping round Thorkel Do-It, wanting to join his crew."

Other men looked round, always quick to spot a quarrel.

Ketil wondered who had told tales on him – but it could have been anyone. The fort was full of gossip.

"I was with the Bisons yesterday," Ketil said. "I'm a free man. I can go where I like."

"And did you ask to join them?"

"Aye. I'm not going to deny it."

In an eye-blink, Eyulf was furious. His face reddened, his eyes glared. Ketil sat up straighter and watched him warily.

"You made a vow to me!" Eyulf said. He put on a whiny voice that was supposed to be Ketil's. "'No man shall ever have cause to rebuke me for leaving this fellowship.'"

"If you'd kept your side of the vow," Ketil said, "maybe I wouldn't want to leave."

Eyulf leaned back and raised his fist – but Ketil raised his own fist and glared back. He'd made up his mind that he was never again going to stand still and be hit.

"So, you don't like our company?" Eyulf said, smiling.

Ketil felt it would be cowardly not to say what he thought. "I don't like all the bickering, and the way you let it go on, and the way you're always picking on the women—"

"Whooo!" went several people, and laughed, but not kindly.

Ketil was angry, and was less careful in choosing his words. "I don't like the way you've got people stealing my things and trying to make a fool of me—"

"*I've* got people doing that?" Eyulf said. "*I'm* always picking on the women?"

"No, but you don't—"

"Hakon!" Eyulf said. "Have I ordered you to make a fool out of Ketil?"

"No," Hakon said, grinning. "I just enjoy it. It's so easy."

"It sounds to me," Eyulf said, "as if your quarrel's with the whole crew."

"No," Ketil said. "It's because—" He wasn't sure how to say what he meant, and started again. "If you kept—" No one was listening anyway.

Eyulf stood. "We should do something to settle it. We should have a holm-ganging."

"Oh aye!" Hakon clapped his hands. Others cheered. Winter, shut up in the fort, was boring. A holm-ganging would be fine entertainment.

"He can't fight us all," Eyulf said, "so we'll make it easy for him. We'll choose a champion. Who'll fight for the crew?"

"Me," Hakon said, grinning at Ketil. "I'll fight him."

"It wouldn't be fair," Eyulf said, "to make this little farm-boy fight a big rough Viking like you.

We should choose a champion he stands a chance against."

Ketil realized where this was going, and he looked for Ottar. He saw him, seated near the open door. Ottar was staring back at him.

"Ottar!" Eyulf said. "As shipmaster, I make you ship's champion, to holm-gang with Ketil."

Ottar tried to say something, but his voice was lost among cheers and laughter from the other men.

A holm-ganging – it meant "island-going" – was a duel. There were hundreds of small islands off the coast of Norway, Shetland and the Orkneys, and in the past holm-ganging had meant just that. The quarrelling men would row out to an island, and fight there. But if there were no islands nearby, then the men marked out a ring and fought within that. It was still called by the old name.

Ottar pushed through the men, keeping his head ducked because of the low roof. Reaching Eyulf, he shouted, "Make someone else champion!"

"I've chosen you," Eyulf said.

"I don't want to do it!" Ottar said.

"Are you breaking your oath too?"

Ottar looked at Ketil, pulling a face as if something was hurting him. Ketil knew Ottar was trying to say that he didn't want to fight him, but had no choice. It made Ketil angrier, because Ottar wanted to stay friends with both sides. *I'm your blood brother*, Ketil thought. *You should side with me against them.*

"I made you the champion to be fair to him," Eyulf said. "I'll make Hakon the champion if you like."

Ottar grimaced at Ketil, and spread his hands, as if to say: *What can I do?*

"Or maybe Ketil would like to back down," Eyulf said, "and admit that we're right – that he whines like a girl and a slave! Do you admit that, Ketil?"

Ketil's anger made his face stiff and cold as the blood left it, quickened his breathing and tightened his muscles. He said, "Hakon, Hrolf, Ottar – I don't care."

"Good!" Eyulf said. "We'll hold it now!"

"Now?" Bjorn said. "Eyulf, what about—?"

"Outside!" Eyulf said.

Men shoved their way out of the dark fellowship hut into the grey daylight, eager to see the fight. Eyulf led the way, Bjorn struggling after him.

Ketil and Ottar were left looking at each other.

Ketil grabbed his axe from his sleeping place, and shoved past. He was angrier by the heartbeat, and felt he would like to hack his way through the whole crew – starting with Ottar.

Outside it was cold, and the men were clearing space for the holm-ganging by moving chests, and logs, and kicking rubbish-dumps flat.

"The square has to be twelve ells on all sides," Hakon said.

"Doesn't matter!" Eyulf snapped. "Big enough for 'em to swing at each other, that's all."

Bjorn was trying to talk to Eyulf, repeating his name over and over – but Eyulf cut him short with a gesture of his hand.

"And there have to be three furrows cut around the square," Bjorn said.

"None of that matters! They're just going to fight," Eyulf said.

They were still arguing, and Bjorn was still trying to have his say, when one of Halfdan's captains came to call them to their work-service.

"*Strider* will be late today," Eyulf told them. "We have something to do first."

"Halfdan's service comes before everything," the captain said.

"It's private business," Eyulf told him; and when the captain argued, he shouted, "We'll come when we've finished here."

The captain left; but men from other crews were gathering. Word had got out, as it always does.

Ketil paced up and down, swinging his axe, full of angry energy. He was eager to get on, get this done with, one way or another— Someone stepped into his way, and he stopped short. It was Ottar, holding a shield and axe.

"I don't want to do this," Ottar said.

Ketil hadn't thought his anger could get worse, but it increased so much it almost choked him. He had to drag in a deep breath before he could say, "I do!" He shouldered past Ottar.

"Ready!" Eyulf called out. He and Hakon had made the onlookers stand back, clearing a space between the fellowship houses.

"It's not big enough," Bjorn said. "If you're going to do this, do it right! There should be posts and ropes or—"

"It'll do!" Eyulf said. "The fight's the thing! Now, Ketil's quarrel is with Strider's whole crew." He walked round the cleared space, shouting this out to everyone there. "He says we've made fools of him, and stolen from him! Ketil, do you maintain this?"

"Aye!" Ketil said. He took his place at one end of the cleared space, and glared at Ottar.

Eyulf pointed out Ottar, standing opposite Ketil. "Ottar has been chosen as ship's champion. The ship accuses Ketil of whining all the time, like a slave-girl; and of wanting to break his vows to me, his shipmaster." There was a slight groan from the watching crowd. "Ottar, do you maintain this?"

Ottar said nothing, but looked away from Eyulf and swung his axe.

"Ottar! As ship's champion, do you maintain that Ketil is a whinging slave-girl?"

Ottar gave a sidelong jerk of his head, and said, "Aye!"

Eyulf turned, looking at the gathered crowd, crammed between the low thatches of the fellowship houses. "Who'll be seconds?" Eyulf demanded.

Bjorn stepped forward. "I'll second Ketil – if he'll have me."

Ketil nodded, and Bjorn came to his side, bringing a shield. It was Bjorn, as second, who would use the shield to protect Ketil from Ottar's blows.

Hakon had gone to Ottar's side, and taken his shield.

Ketil was aware that the crowd were shouting and laughing, but their noise faded from his attention. He was watching Ottar, and tightening and loosening his grip on the shaft of his axe.

"Let Ketil have the first blow," Eyulf said.

Leaving his shield with Bjorn, Ketil walked across the space between him and Ottar. Anger made him want to run and hack, but a fierce, cold control had come to him, and he considered, coolly, exactly how to strike. The rules of holm-ganging said that Ottar wouldn't be able to strike back. Head-blow or leg-blow?

Ketil broke into a run as he made up his mind. He swung the axe high, as if to bring it down on Ottar's head – and Hakon lifted the shield to fend the blow off. Halfway through the swing, Ketil brought the axe down and round, shifting his feet as he did so, and swung the axe in a back-handed blow at Ottar's legs. Hakon was no fool, though, and he brought the shield down. The axe splintered its edge, and Hakon grunted with the effort of holding the shield against the blow.

Ketil backed off, while men laughed, groaned and cheered all round him. He thought: *What if I'd chopped into his legs?* His anger didn't lessen, but turned icy and sick in his belly.

Now Ottar was coming across with his axe.

Ketil stood up straight, thinking that no one was going to call him a coward. But Ottar's blow was a slow, deliberate and obvious stroke at his head, which Bjorn knocked aside easily. The crowd groaned again, and hissed.

Ottar backed off, and it was Ketil's turn again. *This is stupid*, Ketil thought. It could go on for ages, until blood was spilled, or until one of them gave in – and neither could do that. If Ketil gave in, it would be said that he deserved the insults.

Ketil's anger was dying, and with it, his energy. He ran across the space and aimed an axe-swing at Ottar's side. Hakon swung the shield to meet it, and this time, the shield wasn't splintered. The crowd's groans and hisses were louder.

"They're both girls!" someone shouted.

Ottar was coming towards him, axe in hand, looking more worried than anything – when a horn blew, and men from the crowd staggered into the cleared space, so the holm-gangers couldn't see each other. A horse shoved through the crowd, forcing men before it – other horses came behind it. The rider on the leading horse was Halfdan Ragnarsson.

The riders drew rein, and the crowd pressed back to give the stamping horses room. As men recognized Halfdan, the noise dropped away, and they heard more distant sounds – the shouts of men down on the docks, the bawling of penned sheep, birdsong overhead.

Halfdan didn't speak. He sat his horse and looked about him slowly, deliberately, as if studying the face of one man after another. The crowd thinned as men hurried away to their work.

Ketil stood looking up at Halfdan, even meeting his eyes for a moment as the leader glared down. But Halfdan wasn't interested in him, and his eyes moved on. Halfdan wasn't dressed for fighting, Ketil saw, but for hunting. He wore a leather jacket sewn with iron rings, but no helmet, and his greying hair blew about in the wind. There was a bow slung at his back, a quiver of arrows at his saddle-bow; and he carried a spear in his hand.

"Eyulf Thorgeirssen," Halfdan shouted. His voice was always loud, and rough. Eyulf moved forward. "You took an oath to serve me."

"I did, and was proud to do it," Eyulf said.

"Then why are your men here, and not working on my walls?"

"Men have sworn an oath to me, too," Eyulf said, "and I have to give them justice when they ask for it."

Ottar and Ketil looked at each other in surprise.

Halfdan looked around. "Is that what's going on here? The giving of justice?"

"Two of my men had a quarrel," Eyulf said. "They demanded justice from me. So we're having a holm-ganging to settle the matter."

"That's not true!" Ketil shouted, and faces – including Halfdan's – turned towards him. Ketil stepped forward so sharply that Halfdan's horse shied and stamped its forefeet.

"Gently!" Halfdan said. "Are you calling Eyulf Thorgeirssen a liar?"

Ketil caught his breath. Calling a man a liar was a serious thing. He could find himself fighting Eyulf, and Eyulf wouldn't be as half-hearted as Ottar had been. But then his anger quickened again, and he said, "It wasn't like that!"

Eyulf made to speak, but Halfdan silenced him with a gesture. Leaning on his saddle, Halfdan said to Ketil, "What was it like?"

Ketil was scared then. It was like trying to explain himself to a bear, and he didn't think he could do it.

"Answer!" Halfdan said.

"The holm-ganging was Eyulf's idea—"

"To settle your quarrel," Halfdan said.

"No – he was angry with me because I wanted to leave his service."

Halfdan straightened in his saddle, and looked from Ketil to Eyulf and back again. "You wanted to leave his service?"

"Aye!" But suddenly all the objections he had to serving Eyulf seemed childish and petty; and he couldn't find the words to make Halfdan understand. He looked across to Ottar, but Ottar was looking at the ground.

Halfdan said to Eyulf, "Why does this man want to leave your service?"

Eyulf said, "Because he's idle, and doesn't like to work – doesn't like obeying orders – he's one of those men who's always whining and trying to get out of work."

Ottar's head came up sharply, and his mouth opened, but he was beaten to speech by Ketil, who said, "That's not true!" His face flushed, he pointed at Eyulf. "He took an oath to me as well as me to him! He said he'd guard me, and always speak up for me – and he never did! He let all the other men pick on me and Ottar – we had to do all the chores – we got the worst of the food – the worst sleeping places! We didn't mind doing our fair share, but it was never fair! And he let them get away with it. He never spoke up for us. He doesn't keep order in his own crew. He's scared of his men!"

Halfdan grinned, and Ketil felt small. Halfdan thought he was funny, like a toddler in a rage.

Halfdan looked at Eyulf. "This man is unhappy in your service, and you're unhappy with him. Free him, why don't you?"

Eyulf's face was white with anger, but he knew he was being given an order.

Halfdan jerked his head at Ketil. "Give him his token back."

Ketil fumbled to open his pouch, and took out the slip of wood with *Wave Strider*'s sign burned on it. He also found, and handed back, the ring Eyulf had given him. Eyulf took them, and shouted out, "I free you from your oath to me."

The hoofs of Halfdan's horse pounded on the ground as it shifted its weight. "What are you going to do, now you're a masterless man?" Halfdan asked.

"Join the Bison crew," Ketil said.

Halfdan frowned. "Thorkel Do-It. Will he have you?"

"I'll ask him," Ketil said, and half-turned to go, but stopped at a signal from Halfdan's hand. "Stay, stay. Eyulf Thorgeirssen! Play whatever games you like with your crew, but first make sure they've done their day's service to me, and that their antics aren't drawing other men away from their work. I could have been hunting this while, but I had to come, like a captain, and fetch men to their work. I don't like that, Thorgeirssen."

"Aye, Halfdan," Eyulf said. He was furious and shamed but didn't dare say anything but that.

Halfdan stood in his stirrups and bellowed, "Away to your work!"

The few men that had lingered, scattered. Eyulf went too, and Ottar. The muddy passages between the fellowship houses were empty except for Halfdan's mounted hunting party, and Ketil, on foot beside Halfdan's horse.

Halfdan looked down at him. "Do you think you've done a good day's work by breaking your oath?"

"I'm glad to be free of the Wave Striders. And Eyulf. And I didn't break my oath! I ended it."

Halfdan grinned again, then leaned down towards Ketil. He probably thought he was speaking quietly, but his voice was still loud. "Don't end it a second time." Then he straightened, kicked up his horse and rode away.

CHAPTER NINE
Winter's End

OTTAR WAS ALREADY AT TABLE in Halfdan's hall, sitting with the Strider men, when the Bisons sauntered in, led by their big, fair-haired shipmaster. They were in a good mood, waving to friends and laughing. Ketil was with the little red-bearded man called Grim, and Ketil was laughing too.

The sight made Ottar feel sad, and lonely – and angry, and guilty, and so many other things that he couldn't sort out all his feelings. He knew how unhappy Ketil had been with Strider – but still, what a baby to run away, leaving Ottar on his own, just because of a bit of teasing! After they'd sworn blood brotherhood too!

Now all the jokes were on him. It made him realize how much Ketil had put up with, and he felt guilty for not taking Ketil's part more. Too late now.

Hrolf, sitting beside Ottar, called out, "Hey, Ketil! Ketil Faith-Breaker!"

Ketil glanced their way. He saw Ottar, of that Ottar was sure, but before Ottar could smile or nod, Ketil turned away, as if Ottar was a stranger. The Bison men, Ketil with them, found seats somewhere on the other side of the hall, lost in the smoke.

"Dirty little scab," Hrolf said, and others nodded and grunted in agreement.

"Ketil's all right," Ottar said.

"Are you taking your token back as well?"

Ottar pretended he hadn't heard, and looked away. Hrolf laughed.

The Strider men talked about Ketil. Who did he think he was, that he was too good for them? Who was he, the King of Daneland? And what was so great about the Bison fellowship?

"He must be desperate, their shipmaster, if he's got to poach little scabs like Ketil," Hrolf said.

Bjorn told them to give it a rest, but they didn't.

Couldn't. Later, when they stumbled back through the dark to their fellowship house, they saw the men of the Bison ahead of them, and called, "Scab!"

"Faith-breakers!"

Some men of the Bison looked back in surprise, as if they couldn't understand what the noise was about.

Life in the fort during winter was dull. The work on the landward wall was finished, and only a few raiding parties were sent out. If you weren't sent on one of these raids, then there was nothing to do but chores. Men improved their fellowship houses, overhauled the ships, kept the fort defences in repair, polished their armour, practised with weapons. They held wrestling matches, and strength contests – but they were still bored.

Three times Eyulf asked Halfdan to let him take his men raiding, and was refused. He asked why, and Halfdan gave him a long hard look in silence, before saying, "No, Thorgeirssen."

The other Striders soon found an explanation. They blamed Ketil. "That little scab went whining to Halfdan, didn't he? Called Eyulf a liar – said we were picking on him. So now Halfdan doesn't trust us."

After that, they called Ketil "Scabby" all the time, and the men of Bison they called "Scabbies". If a group of Striders met a band of Bisons as they went about the fort, they'd shout, "How are you, Scabbies? Broken faith yet today?"

Grim put his hand on Ketil's shoulder, and said, "Better a scabby Bison any day than a dirty Strider!"

As the jeering went on, it got harder to stand. To Ketil, it was like the chafing of a wet boot on a heel, rubbing at the same place until it rubbed a sore.

The Bison men were outside their fellowship house one night, in the dusk, gathering together before going to the hall. Four Striders called out, "Hello, Scabbies! Broke faith yet today?" And laughed.

Ketil swung round and started after the Striders. Toke and Asgrim laughed and followed his lead. They were going to show the Strider men!

From the dusk behind them came a bellow. "Get back here! Now! Do it!"

Toke and Asgrim stopped. "It's Thorkel," Toke said.

"Ketil!" Asgrim called. "Come back!"

Ketil hesitated and looked back, but he still followed after the Strider men.

"Get back here now! Do it!"

Toke and Asgrim turned back. Ketil came to a halt. He heard laughter ahead of him, and thought the Strider men were laughing at him for being called to heel like a hound. He wanted to plant a good punch on just one of them! Even if he was hurt, it would be good to know that he'd bloodied a Strider nose.

"Ketil!" Thorkel yelled.

Ketil felt the Strider laughter pulling him one way, and Thorkel's voice yanking him back the other. It would be pushing his luck to fall out with another leader.

He started back to Thorkel, feeling as if his feet were made of stone.

Thorkel Do-It stood with folded arms and an angry face, watching him come. He pointed to a spot on the ground in front of him, meaning that Ketil should stand there.

His feet feeling even heavier, Ketil took the step or two to stand right in front of Thorkel.

Thorkel glowered at him, and Ketil felt edgy and twitchy. He tried to explain. "I only—"

Thorkel shoved his face right into Ketil's, so their noses almost touched, and yelled, "What were you going to do, eh?" Thorkel's breath puffed in Ketil's face. It was so frightening, it was almost funny. "Tell me!"

Between anger and fright, Ketil started to shake. He turned his head aside, to avoid Thorkel's breath and angry eyes.

"*Tell me!*" Thorkel yelled.

Ketil tried to speak, but choked. Toke spoke up instead. "We were going to teach them Striders to laugh on the other side of their faces!"

Thorkel swung round and put his face into Toke's. "Oh, you were?" He turned back to Ketil. He stood so close, he was almost standing on Ketil's feet. "Did I tell you to teach anybody anything?" Ketil realized that he was being dared to shove Thorkel away. He didn't dare. "Did I?"

Ketil was shaking now. His heart thumped so hard, he thought it might burst. He couldn't speak.

"*Did* I tell you to do that?" Thorkel yelled in his face.

It went on and on: the same repeated, yelled question. All the other Bison men looked away; all of them glad they weren't being yelled at.

It wasn't going to end until he answered, so Ketil drew a deep, shaky breath, and shouted back, "No!"

"Then what were you playing at, Sheep's-Head? Who is it lives in that hall up there? Remind me. *Answer* me when I ask you a question!"

"Halfdan, Thorkel!" Ketil said. He felt breathless.

"You think Halfdan's going to thank you for starting a fight inside his own fort? Between his own men? Do you?"

Ketil feared he would cry if this went on much longer. "They started it!"

"I didn't see 'em throw a punch."

"They called us—"

"Oh, they called you *names*! They hurt your *feelings*! Oh, shame! What are you?" Thorkel swung round to yell at his whole crew, who all moved back a step and hung their heads. "Are you snot-nosed brats of seven?" he demanded. "Is your dad bigger than their dad? Let me tell you this, all of you." His voice went quiet, and he put his hands on his hips. "Any of you who start a brawl with that scum will answer to me! Eyulf Strider may be happy to lead a crew of sniggering brats, but I expect *my* crew to be men – or, anyway, to try and behave like men. So ignore them! Do it!"

Toke said, "What if they start a fight with us?"

Thorkel said nothing for a moment, just stared until Toke looked away. Then, even more quietly, he said, "You'd better have good witnesses to swear on Thor's Ring that you fought in self-defence, or I'll have you whipped. You're here to fight Saxons, not your own side. Remember that!"

They all trooped to the hall in silence. Ketil felt furious with Thorkel for about twenty paces; and then thought, well, maybe he'd deserved it. He knew one thing: he didn't want to make Thorkel Do-It angry again. Funny how he hadn't cared about annoying Eyulf, even though Eyulf had knocked him down.

They entered the heat and smoke of Halfdan's hall, and had to pass the Striders' table. The Striders threw bits of bread and called names, as usual. Thorkel Do-It, instead of leading the way to empty benches, walked straight towards the Striders. The Bison men all stopped short in surprise.

The Strider men carried on throwing things, and Thorkel was hit by a few crusts. Ketil was shocked. Then he was angry, in the way he'd be angry if someone broke something belonging to him. He ran a few steps, caught Thorkel up, and walked with him.

Thorkel took no notice of the bread that hit him, or even the few bones, and when the Striders saw that he wasn't going to be frightened off, the jeers died away. That made Ketil glad, in an angry way.

Thorkel leaned on the table in front of Eyulf, leaning far over, so he was close to the other man. He just leaned there, in silence, and waited.

Ketil stood beside him, and glared at the Strider men, feeling his anger sharpen because some of them were laughing. Let one of them attack Thorkel, or even look as if they might! The other Bison men came up behind him. What if there was a fight in the hall? Halfdan would punish them all. At that moment, Ketil didn't care.

Eyulf went on talking to the man beside him, pretending that he hadn't noticed Thorkel. Thorkel stayed where he was, and Eyulf couldn't ignore him for ever. Eventually, he looked up and snapped, "What?"

Thorkel said, loudly, "Are you in charge of your men, or do they have you along for decoration?"

Eyulf gaped at him, while all the Strider men

turned to stare. Ketil had to put his sleeve to his mouth, as if wiping it, to stop himself laughing out loud.

Eyulf stood, to be taller than Thorkel. Thorkel straightened, and he was the taller man. He said, "Well?"

"I'm the shipmaster!" Eyulf said.

"I've seen crews pay more attention to the ship's cat!" The Bison men, and many others at nearby tables, laughed aloud. "If you're shipmaster, act like it, and call your men to order!"

Eyulf's face was scarlet. "You can't give me orders!"

"Somebody has to give orders, and you're not doing it! Understand this, friend – if a man left your ship, it was because he was unhappy there, and he was unhappy because you let your men run about, and snap, and spread their fleas, like a lot of cur-dogs."

The men of Wave Strider sat in a row, slack-jawed, astonished that someone would stand in front of them and call them cur-dogs to their faces. One got up, and Ketil and several others of the Bison men stepped forward – but then other Strider men pulled their fellow down into his seat again, with glances towards Halfdan's end of the hall.

"A freeman has a right to leave a leader he's not happy with," Thorkel said, and Ketil felt warm, as if he'd drunk mulled ale, because his new shipmaster was speaking up for him. "If you want to keep your crew, behave like a shipmaster – and keep your flea-bitten curs away from my good hounds!"

Then Thorkel turned his back on Eyulf, and walked away to his own table, his men following.

They half expected the Strider men to attack them as they made their way back to the fellowship house, but nothing happened. And, for a day or two, even the name-calling and jeering stopped.

Then the trouble started again, but there wasn't much name-calling. Instead, things belonging to the Bison men were stolen, or damaged. A hole poked in the roof of their house, food left outside taken, a belt cut in two... Everyone knew who'd done it, because of the grins on the Striders' faces, but it couldn't be proved. So they brought everything inside, left guards, and were careful.

Things quietened as the winter bit down. Frosts, and short, grey days of iron cold were followed by deep snowfalls. The faster parts of the river still flowed, but the backwater where the ships were moored, froze. There was nothing to do but huddle in the warm fellowship houses and play games, and gamble, eat, and tell stories. Ketil was even more glad, during those days, that he had joined Bison. The company of the Striders at such close quarters for so long would have been hateful. Was Ottar enjoying it? he wondered. But it was what Ottar had wanted: to be part of the Great Army.

Chapter Ten

The Monastery

SPRING CAME, SLOWLY. The snow melted, and a dozen little streams chuckled down to swell the river. The days were brighter, and new leaves appeared, though the wind still had a knife-edge. Now the Army would leave its winter quarters. Now it would fight; and win fame, and gold.

The gossip was all about Halfdan's plans. There was a rich monastery on the Isle of Lindisfarne, and Halfdan meant to raid it. He was going to send ships to Pictland, to plunder and take slaves. He was going to send horsemen riding right across the

Saxon lands, to rich Carlisle on the western shore.

The shipmasters went to Halfdan every day, to receive his orders. "Thor and Odin bless us," Asved said, "and let us be sent to Pictland. I should like to be on a ship again. And we'd all get rich."

"Tough fighters, the Picts," Grim said. "I'd sooner fight Saxons and get my gold for less work."

But they weren't sent to Pictland or against Carlisle. Thorkel came back from the stronghold one day and said, "Well, lads, we get to put our feet up, and keep the fire going here while Halfdan's away."

His men groaned and booed.

"Somebody's got to do it," Thorkel said. "We spent all that time building the place, we don't want the Saxons taking it while our back's turned. And here's a laugh – the Striders are keeping us company."

Ketil thought this funny until he heard Asved and Grim talking later. They thought Halfdan was punishing them for their quarrel with the Strider men.

"You can't blame him," Asved said. "Who wants to make war with men who'd rather fight each other than the enemy?"

"He could have sent us to Pictland and the Striders to Carlisle," Ketil pointed out.

"He's letting us know who's king around here," Grim said. "'I give the best chances,' he's saying, 'to men who behave themselves.'"

Asved nodded.

"We didn't do anything wrong!" Ketil said.

The others laughed at him. Only small boys expected things to be fair.

So the Bison men and the Striders stayed in the fort, along with some other crews. They guarded the place, stacked provisions in the store sheds, kept the ships in repair. The two crews ignored each other, even though they were all restless, and bored. They wanted better chances next year; so they made sure that no bad reports of them reached Halfdan.

Many ships left the fort, sailing down the river Tyne, to make war on Pictland; and troops of men on horse and on foot left to march and fight their way over the hills and moors to Carlisle. So both rumours had been true.

Ketil watched them go, and didn't know whether to feel relieved or guilty. Relieved that he could be fairly sure, now, of being alive for the hardships of next winter; or guilty that he'd dragged his Bison friends into the quarrel that had lost them their chance of gold and fame.

But, after all, they got their chance. One day, a captain came to talk with Thorkel. They walked up and down for a long while; and then Thorkel called his men to their fellowship house, to hear what had been said.

During the winter Halfdan's questioning of prisoners had told him of a small Christian monastery to the north-west of the fort. It would have food in store, and fuel; and it might have riches. Even small Christian God-houses often had a bit of gold and silver tucked away. The Bison men were to find the monastery, and bring back its treasure.

"That's more like it!" Asved said. "We get to stretch our legs anyway!"

"We'll be stretching our legs with the Striders," Thorkel said. There was an outcry of disbelief. "Don't blame me! Halfdan's orders."

Ketil couldn't understand why Halfdan had left orders for the Striders and Bisons to find the monastery together. Had he forgotten their feud?

The other men didn't think it strange. "He's the king," Grim said. "'You can't live together and work together?' he says. 'Right, then you'll go into Saxon country together. Learn to work together, or die together.'" Other men nodded. Grim tapped the side of his head and said, "That's how kings think. That's why they're kings and we're—"

"The poor ignorant beggars who pile their treasure-houses full for 'em," Asved finished.

They'd left the fort that morning. Some of the men from each fellowship had stayed behind, to help guard the fort and ships, but there were still eighty men – a strong force.

They passed through the gate of the fort, clunking across the wooden bridge over its ditch. Eyulf and Bjorn, Thorkel and Grim, rode horses, while the rest walked, leading pack-ponies. They had a rough idea of how to find the monastery, but couldn't be sure how long it would take them, so the ponies were loaded with tents and food, as well as arrows and armour.

The two crews weren't together, except that they were travelling in the same direction. Striders and Bisons kept well apart, and although there was no name-calling, or throwing things, they didn't look at each other with any friendliness.

They'd climbed uphill from the river, moving over land that had been cleared of trees and bushes.

On the higher ground was the ruin of an ancient wall, built across the country by the Roman giants, and they followed it at a brisk walk. The way was often steep and rocky, and the riders dismounted and led their horses up in a scramble. The ponies were difficult about coming down some of the steeper paths. Still, it was easier going than on lower ground, where it would be marshy, or wooded.

It was breezy up there too, and the sharp wind kept them cool. They could see for miles on either side, so they couldn't be taken by surprise. They'd see any Saxon war-band coming in plenty of time to get their armour and weapons from the ponies' packs.

The only Saxons they saw were in settlements glimpsed from the ridge. Seeing them, and the smoke rising from roofs, reminded Ketil of his home. He felt it tug at his heart, from all those many miles away.

Ottar was nearby, trudging along with the men of Wave Strider. Maybe he was thinking of Shetland too – but Ketil wasn't going to ask. He and Ottar were no longer of the same fellowship.

Eyulf and Thorkel spoke together now and again. None of the other men did, but they watched each other, and the Bisons quickly noticed how unwilling Eyulf was to dismount from his horse. He rode the poor beast even up the worst slopes, and came near to being thrown a couple of times. His face was furious when he heard the Bisons snigger; and the Striders were angered too. Yet all Eyulf had to do was dismount and walk his horse where the going was hard – as Thorkel had done.

"He's seen that Thorkel's a head taller than him," Grim said, "and he thinks we haven't!" Which set the Bisons guffawing again.

"Shut that noise!" Thorkel said, and glared when one last snort escaped someone.

"Aye, Thorkel," several of them said meekly, and then grinned at each other.

It was midday when Ketil pointed to some buildings in the distance. "Is that the monastery?"

Thorkel called a halt, and they stood shading their eyes and peering at the buildings. There were several of them, built within a round enclosure, and surrounded by fields and woods.

"That building's made of stone," Ketil said. "Painted white. And it's got a cross on the roof."

"Must be it," Thorkel said.

The Striders had gone on along the ridge, but

someone had noticed that the Bisons had stopped. Eyulf came back to them on his horse. "What's wrong?" he demanded.

"Nothing," Thorkel said. "That's the monastery down there. We'll take a rest, have something to eat, and then go down to it."

"We should go on further," Eyulf said.

"Why?" Thorkel asked. "It's more open ground from here to the monastery. We can see further. If you go on, you'll be coming down from the hill into those woods."

"We'll be closer to the monastery, and the woods will give us cover," Eyulf said.

Asved sniggered, and Grim hid a smile. It was clear that, whatever Thorkel suggested, Eyulf would disagree.

"Woods can hide Saxons too," Thorkel said. "No."

Eyulf half-turned his horse. "I'm going on."

"It's a bad idea," Thorkel said, "to split our forces."

"Then follow me," Eyulf said.

Thorkel shook his head. "I'm not taking my men down into those woods."

"I am."

"You go, then," Thorkel said. "I'm staying here."

And then Eyulf had to go on, or look a fool. His men followed him. The Bison men laughed at them, unpacked their bags and settled down to eat and drink. Thorkel stood on the wall, with Grim, studying the land below. Jumping down for his share of food, he said, "We'll arm before we go on."

It was pleasant to sit after hours of walking, to lean against the old stones in the sun, and eat, talk and laugh. For that short while Ketil was able to forget why he was there. It was almost like being back home, resting from field-work.

Thorkel didn't let them rest for long. "On your feet! Arm!"

They unpacked their gear quickly, without talk. Things were serious now. Ketil found his long, thick leather coat, and pulled it on over his tunic and breeks. Around him, others were pulling on similar coats. Thorkel was the only man with a mail coat. Ketil didn't envy him the heavy thing. He'd rather not have all that weight hanging on his shoulders as he slogged over to the monastery.

Thorkel, Grim and one other man had helmets. All the others had leather caps, or nothing at all.

Those that had swords belted them on, and slung their shields on their backs. They took up spears, axes, bows. Ketil had a bow, and a heavy quiver of forty arrows. As they started down from the ridge, some men were carrying two axes, or two lots of spears, leaving others with hands free, to manage the horses.

Ketil was scared now. It was harder to walk with the extra weight of leather jacket, shield and quiver; and he was carrying that extra weight because they were in greater danger. They were leaving the ridge, where they'd been able to see anyone coming, and going down into the fields. Down there, thickets, walls and even dips in the ground could hide the enemy from them. He prayed to Thor and Frey for protection.

The monastery had seemed close from the top of the ridge, but once they were on lower ground, it disappeared. They had a hot, sweaty trudge to reach it. Sweat collected under Ketil's leather cap, and he lugged at his heavy shield. The quiver thudded against his back. He tried to forget all that and keep his eyes moving from side to side of the path, into the bushes and trees, up to the skyline. Did something move there? What was that noise? He caught his breath a few times, and his heart banged, sure that a huge, screaming Saxon was about to charge at him with down-driving axe.

But it was a boar that had shouldered aside bushes, disturbed by the men.

He wondered where all the Saxons had gone. But then, he was one of forty men, all armed, and not quiet. They tramped along, shields chafing on shoulders, scabbards thumping on legs, breath grunting. The locals must know they were there, and were keeping out of the way. Why would swineherds and shepherds rush to fight them?

It was after midday when they came in sight of the monastery again. They stopped at the top of a small hill, sparsely wooded with birch. Hot, sweaty, panting, they looked down into a gentle little valley folded into the hills. The monastery was a collection of thatched, wooden buildings surrounding a small stone church. Its low, circular wall was of earth, topped with hurdles.

Around the monastery there were ploughed fields, a small orchard…

"Animal pens," Ketil said. "Pigsty, henhouses."

A small stream had been dammed to form a fish pond.

"Plenty of food, anyway," came Thorkel's voice. "We could eat well tonight, lads."

Ketil said, "There are men in the pigsty."

Thorkel heard, and came to stand by him. "What?"

Moving slowly, Ketil pointed and, as Thorkel looked, there was a dull flash – the afternoon light reflecting from a spear point. There – now they looked carefully – were the crouched shapes of men in the pigsty.

"And look," Ketil said. "At the corner of the building there..."

Sunlight was throwing a shadow from behind a building over a piece of open ground. It was distorted, but it still looked like a man with a spear.

"You've good eyes," Thorkel said. "And look there."

Ketil followed Thorkel's slight nod. Beyond the monastery was a lightly wooded slope – and coming down through those trees were armed men, carrying shields, spears and axes.

"Eyulf!" Grim said. "They must never have stopped to draw breath!"

"Planning to get ahead of us," Thorkel said, "and grab everything – and all the glory as well!"

"He's going to get a surprise," said Grim.

Scattered along the hillside, in the thin cover of

the trees, the Bison men watched Eyulf's men leave their cover and cross the open ground towards the monastery.

Thorkel's men glanced towards him, as if wondering why they weren't moving themselves, but Thorkel stood watching, and grinning.

Ketil saw Ottar among Eyulf's men. He was smaller than the others, and Ketil knew his movements. There he was, the other Shetland lad, with his leather coat and cap, his heavy shield, and an axe in his hand – not coming last, but struggling to keep up with the leading men, with their longer strides.

And there were the Saxons, waiting in the monastery.

"Aren't we going to help them?" Ketil said.

"They worked hard for this," Thorkel said. "Let 'em have it."

They stood and watched. Thorkel's men sniggered. Someone whispered, "Come on the Saxons!" and there was muted laughter.

Ketil found himself grimacing, as if in pain, as he watched Eyulf's men move closer to the small ditch and low wall that surrounded the monastery. He reminded himself that he and Ottar had fallen out;

and that the Strider men had tormented him. Why should he care what happened to them?

He leaned on a tree and watched as Ottar jumped down into the shallow ditch; and as the leading man climbed from the ditch towards the low wall.

What if Ottar was maimed or killed? What if, when he went home, he had to tell Ottar's parents that he'd idly watched as Ottar was killed? Not that he would say that. He'd lie. But whatever he told them, he'd know the truth himself.

As one man was awkwardly straddling the wall, and as others were in the ditch, the hidden Saxon men leaped, yelling, to their feet, and threw spears.

The Northmen, startled by the yells, froze, half-ducked, and then saw Saxons running at them, screaming, raising axes—

Ketil was startled – by the laughter of the Bison men around him.

Ketil grabbed up his bow and his spear, and ran out of the trees, down the hill, towards the monastery.

Behind him, Thorkel yelled, "That man! Back here! Do it!"

Ketil didn't even hear him. He dropped his spear and raised his bow – it was already strung. He took an arrow from his quiver and nocked it to his string, while watching the fight below. Had they seen him? His flesh cringed from the imagined impact of arrow-point or axe-edge – the hair on the back of his neck rose in anticipation of it, and his fingers fumbled.

He drew up, but released too soon, and badly. The arrow didn't travel far. He nocked on another, and loosed again. The Northmen and Saxons had met now. He heard the thump and rattle and crack of axe on shield and head and leg – the yells and grunts.

Ketil drew up and loosed, drew up and loosed, falling into the unthinking rhythm Grim had drilled into him. Three arrows in the air, and one on the string. Up the arrows sped, vanishing against the sky – and then fell from the air onto the Saxons, startling them, scaring them…

Draw up, loose. Draw up, loose. It was like hunting, he was so calm…

Chapter Eleven
Looting the Monastery

OTTAR'S THUMPING HEART felt huge, filling his chest and throat, shaking and choking him. This was his first real fight. His heavy leather coat dragged at his shoulders. His sweaty hand slipped on the haft of the axe he would soon have to use. His shield was so heavy – heavy, but too thin... A flash of memory showed him Ketil, in play, hacking and pounding at his shield, and his heart pummelled in his throat and belly until he could hardly breathe...

"There'll only be a few of their 'monks'," Eyulf had said. "On their knees, praying. They won't fight.

We'll get a bit tired chasing 'em, that's all."

Ottar feared that he wouldn't be able to chop at a kneeling man, as he would chop at a block of wood. He'd seen himself, in his mind, hacking down men as easily as a farmer cut down corn stalks with a sickle. But now, it seemed more like butchering a pig. The axe would judder against flesh, and whack against bone; the man would scream and thrash; the oily blood would pour...

Ottar was afraid that he would stand there while others did the fighting; and he would be shamed.

With luck, he'd be killed, and wouldn't have to face his fellows afterwards.

But he was afraid that dying would be hard, and painful, and he'd die a coward.

But still he walked towards the monastery, because he was afraid to be the only one who didn't. He prayed to Thor and Frey, and any God who might listen: *Keep me safe...*

Ahead of him was the shallow ditch that surrounded the monastery, and beyond that, the low wall. Hrolf was scrambling out of the ditch and raising one leg to climb the wall —

Ottar didn't know what the shouting was – angry, guttural shouting – he wasn't even sure where it came from. He stood still, in the ditch, gaping round, wondering—

There were men on the *other* side of the wall. Men yelling. Men with shields. They didn't look much like what he'd heard of Christian monks.

A spear went by him. He watched it – a long spear that thudded into the grass. He thought: *That was thrown at me* – and he didn't know which way to run.

Looking up, he saw Hrolf fall backwards, and a shouting man coming over the wall with a spear. There were other men, coming over the wall, yelling—

A yell from beside him, and Ottar saw Strider men shouting and running forward, shields up, axes and swords in hand. Ottar put up his shield, grasped the haft of his axe in a slippery hand, and went forward with them, clambering out of the ditch—

And while he was still, awkwardly, half in the ditch, there was an axe above him—

Grabbing up his spear, Ketil ran further down the slope, stabbed his spear into the ground and shot again. He was close to the fight now, and had to change his aim, but his arrows struck with greater force. A man hit in the arm was spun round.

He ran still closer. By moving often, he made his arrows fall from different directions, maybe fooling the Saxons into thinking there was a troop of archers hidden in the trees.

From the monastery came a crash of iron on wood, an outcry of voices, but Ketil, drawing up, aiming and loosing, drawing up, aiming and loosing, hardly heard it…

"Trolls take me!" Thorkel said, as the Bisons watched Ketil attack alone. He looked round at his men, drew his sword, raised it and shouted, "Do it!"

With spears, axes, swords, hammers, the Bison men charged.

For Ketil, it was as if he and Ottar had never fallen out. He was angry that anyone dared to threaten his friend. He was scared too – but both the anger and fear were distant, held away from him and tightly controlled. He concentrated, drawing up, aiming and loosing with the same movements again and again. It was the best shooting he'd ever done.

A man swiped at Ottar's head, and Ottar folded into the ditch. Ketil yelled in rage, snatched up his spear and ran towards Ottar, his bow in his other hand, his heart thumping —

The man who had hit Ottar turned away from him and ran on, already swinging his axe to chop at someone else. Ketil jumped into the ditch and ran along it, reaching Ottar and standing astride him. He dropped his bow, wrenched the shield from Ottar's arm, and, as he fitted the shield on his own arm, spun around to see if anyone was near him. There were men nearby. Stooping, Ketil grabbed up Ottar's axe.

He saw the Bison men running from the trees and yelled, "Bison!" – turning back to the fight in time to see something swinging at him.

He didn't even know that he had moved his shield to block the blow until he felt the jar go through his bones, crashing down through his spine. He heard the wood of his shield splintering, and only escaped being knocked from his feet by bowing under the blow and going into a deep crouch.

Under the shelter of his shield, he glimpsed a pair of booted legs – the legs of the man who had struck at him. With the axe in his hand he struck at the legs clumsily, without any real thought – as a toddler slaps back at another toddler who has slapped him.

It wasn't the hardest or best-aimed blow, but it was struck with a sharp axe, and brought a cry of pain and rage from the man, who stumbled backwards.

Ketil sprang upright from beneath his shield, already swinging his axe up and round. He brought it down on the fallen man, who blocked with his shield, but late, so Ketil's axe bit into its edge, and sent a chunk flying.

Ketil swung up his axe again, bringing it down once, twice, beating the shield into the face of the man sheltering under it, smashing it. The man tried to hit Ketil with his sword, but he was badly placed and had no luck.

Another blow, and the shield would be firewood, and the man crow-meat – but then there were heavy footsteps and hard breathing close by, and Ketil jumped back, turning to defend himself against this newcomer—

Who was Thorkel Do-It. Without a glance at Ketil, he rammed his sword into the belly of the man on the ground, and twisted the blade to free it from the grip of the flesh. He gave Ketil one look, eyes glittering in the shadows of his helmet, and ran on.

Ketil, breathless and shaking, stumbled back, away from the Saxon on the ground. Ottar was on his knees, but unable to stand. He tried, and collapsed again, like a piece of string.

Ketil stood astride him. His heart racketed, and his legs shook. He turned his head constantly, trying to watch all sides, and was jolted again and again by surges of alarm as some movement or sound made him think attack was near. All his muscles, in his arms and legs and back, jumped and twitched with weariness and effort.

The fight had moved away from him – a tangle of men hacked and shoved, shouldered and slashed in and around the monastery's ditch and wall, with grunting and panting, bashing, splintering, clashing. Ketil thought he ought to join the fight – but that would leave Ottar undefended.

Ottar struggled to sit. He looked up at Ketil, his face unrecognizable, coated over as it was with blood from his head-wound. Ottar's eyes blinked through the blood, but he said nothing.

A Saxon ran at them, his feet pounding on the earth and his breathing sounding like tearing cloth.

Ketil half-crouched, hefting his axe and bringing up what was left of his shield – but the man ran past – running for his life.

And these men coming towards them were Bison men. The tall man in the lead, wearing a helmet, could only be Thorkel Do-It. Ketil called out, "Have we won?"

Thorkel tugged off his helmet, showing his red and sweating face. His hair stuck up in damp clumps. "Aye, we've won!" He was out of breath. He came up and looked at the Saxon, who was either dead or unconscious. "We'll have that helmet," he said.

Grim kneeled by the Saxon and wrenched the helmet off the man's head. The man moaned, so Grim drew his dagger and cut his throat.

Thorkel went to Ottar and pulled off the leather cap he wore. Putting his sword on the grass, he looked briefly at Ottar's wound, stretching and pulling at his scalp. Ottar hissed, but made no other sound. "Not as bad as it looks," Thorkel said and, taking Ottar by one hand, hauled him to his feet.

Ketil picked up Thorkel's sword and gave it back to him. Thorkel nodded his thanks, and pulled at Ottar's arm. "Come on." To all his men he yelled,

"Don't put your feet up! We've a monastery to loot."

Ottar went with Thorkel, giddily stumbling along. Ketil followed. They walked around the ditch, passing bodies and dying men – several of them Strider men – until they reached the gateway. A narrow earth bridge crossed the ditch, and a wooden gate had been built into the wall of stone and turf. A small bell hung from a gatepost, for visitors to ring for admittance. Grim reached out a bloodied hand and rang it loudly before they went through the gate, which raised a laugh.

Opposite the gate was a tall church, richly built in stone, with a paved area before it. To either side of the church, and behind it, were other substantial buildings, their lower levels of stone, and the upper ones of wood, with low, overhanging thatches. Behind those, other buildings could be glimpsed: a barn, a byre, a stable, henhouses. Ketil, looking about with a farmer's eye, thought it looked a prosperous little place.

The Bison and Strider men had herded prisoners together in front of the church. Some Saxon warriors, taken alive in the fighting, had been made to kneel, and the mail coat and helmet of one lay beside him.

It was the monks Ketil most wanted to see. They were men of all ages, he saw, and women too. Some were dressed in long, plain grey tunics with belts of rope; but others were dressed like nobles. All the male monks had bald patches.

As Thorkel came up, one of the woman stepped forward to meet him. She was a tall, handsome, middle-aged woman, wearing a dark-red tunic fastened at the shoulders with large gold brooches. Her headdress was of fine white linen, secured with a gold pin. Clasping her hands, she looked up at Thorkel, and spoke. Her accent was strange, and Thorkel frowned, not understanding her. But Saxon speech wasn't so different from their own, and when she repeated herself, he understood. She said, "You are welcome to this place of God."

Thorkel laughed aloud, but the woman stood her ground. She spoke again, her voice tight, as if she struggled to control it. "I am Ethelgitha, Abbess of this place, and of noble blood. I am a king's daughter."

Thorkel grinned. "Which king would that be, Lady? Halfdan's tame little king? Or one of the others running about the place, snapping at each other?"

The Abbess said, "We will gladly care for any of your men who are hurt; and we will gladly feed you. Gladly, for the sake of our God. All we ask is that you do no more hurt to anyone here, and respect this holy place."

Thorkel found her amusing, and grinned at his men, who laughed. "That's kind of you, Lady," Thorkel said, and pulled Ottar forward. "Look after him, then! Understand? Look after him – do it!"

The Abbess moved close to Ottar, and examined his head. If she was a king's daughter, she didn't mind getting her hands bloody. Looking up at Thorkel again, she said, "I need to take him to the infirmary."

Thorkel didn't understand the word, but nodded, and then pointed to a couple of his men. "Go with her." He turned to yell at them all. "Anybody else hurt? Limp off with our princess here, then, or get yourself carried."

Ottar and some others limped off with the Saxon woman. Bjorn Strider was one of them, Ketil saw. He had a gashed calf.

Thorkel moved a few paces to left and right, to see round the church, and spotted some men coming from one of the long buildings.

"Are they Strider men?" he demanded. "Get them over here."

"They're searching the buildings, Thorkel," somebody said.

"Who told them to? Get them over here – do it! I want everyone except the wounded here." Men ran to round up the Strider men, and he yelled after them, "Tell them Eyulf's dead! And Bjorn's wounded! So they're my men now, and I'll have the skin off any man who starts looting before I say so!"

"Eyulf's *dead*?" Ketil said.

Thorkel, turning back, leaned towards him and shouted, so that Ketil leaned back, as if from a wind. "Aye, young Ketil, your mate Eyulf's got a spear through him over there. Now, if you've all had enough gossip! We're staying here the night, and we need to keep out passing Saxons and other vermin! Any ideas?"

There were, and Ketil helped drag benches, table-boards and trestles from inside the monastery, and pile them in the narrow gaps between the buildings, making an inner wall inside the low outer one. A couple of carts were heaved out of a shed, and overturned to make part of the barricade; and cupboards and bed-frames found and piled up too, together with hurdles, and stall-partitions torn from the byre and stables; even doors and shutters. They packed gaps with logs from the woodpile, straw-filled mattresses, turfs, stones – anything to make their wall stronger.

The barrier complete, Thorkel posted guards, carefully choosing them from both Strider and Bison men. "I make no favourites," he said. "Keep your eyes peeled, all of you – if you don't, your hides will pay."

The rest of the men, he led back to the church. "Bring the prisoners here. Where's King Dung-Heap's daughter? Her too."

The prisoners were brought: five monks, five nuns, including the Abbess, and three captured warriors. Thorkel looked them over. "King Dung-Heap's daughter's for ransom," he said. "Nobody's to touch her. Aye?" There was a muttered agreement from his men. "Anybody who does will answer to me." He grabbed one young nun by the arm – she gave a squeak of fright – and pushed her towards the Abbess. There was another nun, slightly older, and he pushed her that way too.

Two nuns were left, both elderly women. Thorkel, with a gesture, told them to move to the other side of the paved area. Uncertainly, looking towards their Abbess, they did so.

"Why do you send them over there?" the Abbess called out.

Thorkel ignored her. He was looking the monks over. One was old, and he pointed at the man, and then pointed at the elderly women. The old man shuffled across to them.

All three of the Saxon warriors were young, but one had a gash above his knee, and could hardly stand. "Shame," Thorkel said, but pointed him towards the old man and the old women. "Hog-tie the other two." He looked at the four young monks. "Them too." Then he turned to the Abbess. "Lady, you offered to feed us. Good. But small beer. Nothing stronger." He pointed to two of his men. "You two, go with them." He waved the Abbess and her young nuns on their way.

The Abbess didn't move. "What will you do with my people?"

"Not your business, Lady."

"They are my people. I must know."

Thorkel sighed, and looked at the men he'd appointed to guard the nuns. "Make sure she doesn't serve anything stronger than small beer. Anybody gets drunk, you two'll answer for it."

One of the guards took the Abbess's arm, and hustled her away. The other guard bundled along the older of the two nuns, and the younger scurried after them.

The Abbess struggled against her guard, shouting, "Don't hurt them! Oh, Lord God—" She was dragged around the corner of the church.

Thorkel watched her go, and gave a nod, which Ketil thought was approving. Then he turned to the old people, and the wounded Saxon. He picked out some of his own men, by pointing. "You, you, you and you. Kill them."

Ketil was shocked. Kill the old women? He saw Thorkel looking at him, and tried to pull his face straight.

"Be thankful I haven't told you to do it," Thorkel said.

The wounded Saxon was sitting on the ground. One of the Bison men dragged his head back by his hair. Ketil looked away.

"They're worth nothing as slaves," Thorkel said, "and we've got to get back to the fort yet. The slaves we've got'll be enough to manage. No point struggling with people we can't sell."

"You could let them live!" Ketil said.

Thorkel laughed, as if at a joke, and shoved Ketil towards the other side of the church. "Leave them alive, to run off and tell tales on us?" He waved for men to follow them. Ketil didn't look back.

Thorkel set them to searching the buildings. Ketil threw himself into it, to forget what was happening at the church. There were a couple of well-fed riding horses in the stable...

"We'll have them," Thorkel said.

The pigsty was empty, but there were spindly cattle in the byre. They'd come through the winter on short rations, and weren't strong enough yet to be turned out into the fields.

"Leave 'em," Thorkel said. "I'm no cattle-drover."

There was a henhouse, with a few fowl. "Find a basket to pack 'em in," Thorkel said. "We could do with a few chooks."

In the building next to the kitchens they found silver plates and candlesticks, and drinking horns trimmed with gold. There was a big book, too, on a stand; and the book's cover was studded with precious stones and had a golden clasp.

There were more valuables in the long house filled with beds: bedcovers, bed curtains, candlesticks, and a beautiful green glass jug with a silver base and handle. "Wrap it up well," Thorkel said.

The best pickings were from the church. There were statues in there, wearing golden crowns, necklaces, brooches and rings, all studded with precious stones. They smashed the statues, and took the gold. There were bundles of fine cloth, gold and silver bowls, jugs and candlesticks. There was a casket of gold, with enamel patterns, and garnets and moonstones. When they opened it, there were bones inside, so they threw them away. There was another big book, with gold, gem-studded bands around it, and a jewelled clasp. They tore off all the gold and gems, and threw the book down.

Asved and Hakon broke open a chest in the Abbess's house, and found gold and silver coin, armbands, rings, brooches... The Saxons were a rich people, and all this treasure, and the slaves, made the raiders' long walk and the fight worthwhile.

It was dark now, and Thorkel checked on the men guarding the barricades, before clapping his hands together and saying, "Now for some food, drink, a fire and some female company!"

"Leave some for us," one of the men on guard called out pathetically.

"I shall have your share meself," Thorkel called back.

The Abbess had set out the food in the long building by the kitchens. All the tables and benches had been used in the barricades, so she'd laid the food on the broad stone ledges of the windows. There was bread and strong cheese, apples, dried fish, butter and porridge.

"I am sorry the food isn't better," the Abbess said to Thorkel, "but we had little time."

"We're hungry, there's plenty, and it's good," he said. "Let me taste the beer." When he was satisfied that the beer was weak, he ate with his men, standing up. The Abbess and her two nuns carried round the tub of ale, and ladled it into the men's drinking horns, straining it through a little sieve, to get rid of the thick, porridgy grain it was brewed from.

Ketil was starving, ate quickly, and was barely beginning to feel full when Thorkel hammered an iron ladle on the wall, and pointed out the men who were to stand guard, while the men outside came in to eat. Ketil was one of them.

"I shall come out sometime to check on you, and Thor Himself won't save you if I catch you napping."

Outside, away from the lamplight, it was full,

blinding dark; and the air had the sharp bite of early spring. The men going out passed the men coming in, and were told that they'd taken their time filling their bellies. "I hope the Saxons get you!"

Ketil took his place at the barricade between the eating-hall, and the henhouses. As his eyes became used to the dark, he could see the hurdles and doors piled up. Beyond them, nothing. It was too dark. Anything and anyone might be out there. The barricade seemed a low, flimsy thing.

He could hear the men who'd gone off guard, laughing and shouting in the hall beside him. For a time, they even sang.

He walked up and down his length of barricade, to try and keep warm, feeling an odd mixture of boredom and fear. He heard a footstep behind him, and was so startled, he jumped off the ground. Saxons behind him? He spun round, thrusting out his spear. "Who's there?"

"Me!" said an alarmed voice – Ottar's voice.

Ketil relaxed. "You," he said, and turned away to peer into the darkness beyond the barricade.

Ottar stood beside him. Ketil ignored him, but Ottar still stood there. It became annoying, so Ketil said, "What do you want?"

Ottar coughed. "We're on the same side now."

"We always were."

"I mean – Thorkel says, we're all Bison men now."

"So?" Ketil said.

Ottar said, "Grim told me the Bisons were going to watch the Saxons kill us. He said if you hadn't come charging down on your own, they wouldn't have moved. He said they only joined in to save you."

Ketil was glad it was dark, and hard to see his face. He made a big show of being on guard, peering out at the countryside. He felt glad and proud that the Bison men had wanted to save him. "So? I'm one of the Bison fellowship." He knew what Ottar meant, and what he wanted to say, but he wasn't going to help him. He'd run to save Ottar because – well, because they were blood brothers. He hadn't wanted to see Ottar killed by Saxons, but that didn't mean they could be friends again.

Ottar stood there, in the chill dark, for a long time. His head throbbed, and the food he'd eaten sat uneasily in his belly. His arms and legs were shaky, and he felt desperately tired. What he wanted to say was so difficult. He could go back to the hall, but...

"We could be friends again."

Ketil didn't seem to hear. Ottar waited a while, then swallowed and asked, through a thick throat, "Couldn't we? Be friends again?"

No! Ketil wanted to say. When Ketil had wanted Ottar to be a friend, he'd been none. He opened his mouth to speak the "no", but it stuck in his throat. Maybe they could be friends again... If he could forget the way Ottar had let him down. He didn't know if he could. Or should.

He said, "I'm on guard. You shouldn't be here. Thorkel will have your guts – so clear off."

Ottar still stood there, but Ketil refused to look at him again, or speak.

After a long while, Ottar went back to the hall, where at least it was warm.

CHAPTER TWELVE

Look Out

THORKEL EVENTUALLY SENT out men to relieve those on guard, and Ketil stumbled through the dark to one of the monastery's halls. It felt hot inside after the chill, and a smouldering fire cast a red light.

The men of the previous watch had made themselves beds on the floor, with straw, blankets, furs and lengths of cloth, all taken from the monastery. Ketil found himself a bed, and wrapped himself in blankets and his cloak.

It was hard to sleep. Every time he dozed, he'd

see the axe swinging at him again, and start awake. Or he'd be trying to stand on wounded legs; and then feel the whack of a blow at the back of his own neck – and start awake. He'd see Saxons coming to kill him, and try to run, but be unable to move – until he started awake, sweating.

He was glad when Thorkel's yells broke in on his confused dreams. "Get up! Do it!" All around him, men blearily crawled from their bedding.

The nuns had breakfast ready: porridge with honey, and bread baked only the day before, with butter. It was good, and Ketil ate hungrily.

The Abbess and her two nuns were bareheaded now, their hair loose. The younger two were dressed in blankets, fastened with pins, and one had a bruised face and arms.

After breakfast, Thorkel set men to loading the pack-ponies, and the monastery's horse, mule and donkey, with everything valuable or useful. There was so much, and some of it so heavy, that they couldn't take it all.

"Leave that, leave that," Thorkel said, pointing to one sack and kicking another. He chose to take all the precious metals and jewels. "That's what we're here for – to get rich." Thorkel spun round.

"Where's Ketil? And that other lad?"

Ketil and Ottar came forward. Thorkel stooped to look into Ottar's face, and said, "You'll do. Come with me. Asved! You too!"

Thorkel led the way to the long building behind the church – the place where the monks and nuns had slept at night. They climbed to the upper floor. "I want you lads up there." Thorkel pointed to the cross-beams beneath the thatch. "Break through the thatch, have a good look round."

"What for?" Ottar asked. He must still have been feeling the effects of his bash on the head.

"Pretty girls!" Thorkel said. "What do you think, Sheep's-Head?"

Asved said quietly, "Saxons."

Thorkel stood under the cross-beam, crouched and cupped his hands. Ketil stepped onto them, and was thrown up – it was a bit like flying – and grabbed hold of the beam, disturbing lots of dust. He twisted and hauled himself astride the beam, sitting hunched in the small space under the thatch while he cut through it with the knife from his belt. He coughed in the dust, and the smell of old heather. Tufts of thatch, the wooden pegs that held it, and many beetles, showered onto the floor.

Ottar was struggling onto the beam at the other side of the central post, having been boosted up by Asved.

Ketil broke through to cool, fresh air, and stood on the beam, though he was precariously balanced. He leaned on the peak of the roof above him, and looked about as colour crept into the early morning greyness. The little clearing round the monastery was empty. There wasn't even a sheep.

But there were woods all round. In places, Ketil could see between widely spaced trees; and the branches were, mostly, still bare. He couldn't see anyone, but it was hard to be sure. There were thickets of briar and scrub in places. "Nothing," he shouted.

Ottar's head emerged from the thatch on the other side. "See anyone?" Ketil asked him.

Ottar took time to scan the woods on his side. "No. But there are places men could hide."

From below, Thorkel called, "Stay up there. Keep watch. If a mouse moves, I want to know."

Thorkel and Asved went away, and left Ketil and Ottar perched in the thatch. The beam they stood on was broad enough, but slippery with dust; and they had to stand in much the same position all the time. But it was an important job, and they kept alert, searching with their eyes.

Every now and then Ketil heard Ottar sigh behind him, or shift awkwardly on the cross-beam. He remembered Ottar's apology the night before, and how he'd refused it. He'd thought himself in the right, but now he wasn't so sure.

Twisting towards Ottar, he said, "You call yourself my blood brother, but as soon as things got hard, you dropped me and ran after Eyulf and Hakon and Hrolf."

It was so long before Ottar answered that Ketil thought the breeze had carried his voice away. He tried to see Ottar, but it was difficult to catch more than a glimpse of him. But then Ottar said, "I'm sorry for that."

"All right, then," Ketil said, but still didn't know where they stood. Were they friends, as they'd been before? Or were they like new-met friends, now? Ready to like each other, but with the friendship yet to be tested? He was trying to think how to put this into words, when Ottar said, sharply, "There!"

"What?"

"There!" Ottar said. "Look there!"

Ketil twisted round as far as he could, and tried to

look over the peak of the thatch, in the direction Ottar was pointing. "What?"

"Something flashed. Something metal."

Ketil turned right round on his beam, and leaned on the thatch. He peered into the trees, his eyes wide. He felt that, in another moment, his ears might stand up on top of his head, like an alerted hunting dog's.

"There!" Ottar said.

"Ah!" Ketil saw it too – a fierce flash of sunlight from something metal – a spear-point, or a helmet or shield-fitting... Of course, it could be some woodman with a little wood-chopping hatchet...

"I see him!" Ketil pointed. The figure of a man had jumped from the confusion of twigs, branches and shadows. He could see the hump of his shoulder, and the shield on it. Where there was one man with a shield, there would be many more.

"Aye!" Ottar said, excitedly, and vanished under the thatch. "I'm going to tell Thorkel!"

When it was Ketil who'd first seen the man clear! He crouched, awkwardly getting hold of the beam below him, and dropped to the floor below. Ottar had already gone. Ketil ran after him.

Chapter Thirteen
Ambush

THEY FOUND THORKEL in the long hall where they'd eaten the night before, watching the surviving Strider men lay their dead fellows in rows on the earth floor. Their shields were placed over them, and their weapons by their sides.

Ottar ran up, shouting, "In the woods – Saxons – we saw—"

"Whisht!" Thorkel held up his hands for quiet.

Ketil said, "There are men in the trees, with weapons and shields."

"Where?" Thorkel said. "How many?"

Ottar said, "There was one, but we couldn't see, there might—"

Ketil pointed. "We only saw one man for sure. Over there. But he had some kind of weapon – we saw the sun flash on it. And he had a shield. So he's not on his own, is he?"

Thorkel nodded and, beckoning them to follow, led them out into the yard, where Grim was seeing the slaves tied together. Armed men were guarding them, while others tied their hands. Longer lengths of leather rope were tied from neck to neck, so the slaves had to walk in step with one another, or be choked when the ropes pulled tight. Even the Abbess, the king's daughter, was tied into the line. Each slave was worth between eight and twelve ounces of silver, depending on their age, strength and health.

The sight of the Abbess being tied into line struck Ketil as pitiable, despite the alarm he felt about the Saxons in the woods. Yesterday she'd been a rich and powerful woman. Now she was a slave. The others, too – they might not have been the children of kings, but they'd been free. Now they could be bought and sold, like sheep or dried fish.

He could be enslaved himself, if captured. Would it be better, he wondered, to be killed?

Thorkel told Grim about the Saxons in the wood. "How many rebel Saxons can there be around here?" Grim said. "We already gave one lot a beating. There can't be that many. We've still got seventy fit men."

"Maybe," Thorkel said. "But if there's armed men in the woods – and they haven't come at us openly – then they're planning an ambush, aye?"

Grim thought it over, then nodded.

"There might be enough of 'em to hurt us, if we leave this place. And if we stay here— "

"They'll burn us out," Grim said.

Ketil and Ottar looked at each other. If the monastery was set on fire, the damp thatch might take a while to catch, but it would burn. Every building would burn. They'd be roasted to death. If they tried to escape, the Saxons would be waiting.

Thorkel walked further from the slaves. Grim and the boys followed. Thorkel said, "They don't know that we know they're there… Do you think they know how many we are?"

"They might," Grim said.

"Can't be helped," Thorkel said, folding his arms and shaking his head. "Why are they here? What are they hoping for?" He turned and looked back at the slaves. "Do you think it's Princess Dung-Heap they want? This Saxon out here – he's the local thane, aye? Is Princess Dung-Heap his auntie? Or his mammy?"

Grim shrugged. "Maybe."

"Can we bargain with 'em? Give us safe passage, and we'll give you – what's she called again?"

"The Abbess," Ottar said.

"*Are* we going to give 'em the Abbess?" Grim asked, surprised.

Thorkel snorted with contempt. "Spit on that!"

"It goes like this, then," Grim said. "If we give 'em the Abbess here and now, they let us go a little way, then ambush us anyway. If we say, give us safe passage, and we'll give you the Abbess when we're in sight of the fort – well, would you believe us?"

Thorkel laughed. "They'd be fools if they did! Worth a try?"

"Depends how much time you want to waste," Grim said.

"We could ambush *them*," Ketil said.

Thorkel and Grim looked at him. They seemed amused. Ketil thought he'd see how hard they'd laugh once they'd heard him out. "They think we don't know they're there. So they think we'll come trotting out, with our ponies and slaves. So we do. We go out, but we have axes and swords ready on the ponies. And somebody's up in the rafters, where we were, on watch. And the rest of our men are hiding behind the barricades in here. And when the Saxons come for our men—"

"We grab the swords and axes off the ponies!" Ottar said excitedly.

"Aye," Ketil said. "And while the Saxons are busy fighting, the man on watch shouts, and the rest of us – we run out to attack them as well." He looked at Thorkel and Grim, to see what they thought. He felt breathless, anxious about the fight to come, and anxious that the men shouldn't think him a fool. "Take them by surprise," he added.

Thorkel and Grim stared, then looked at each other.

"You never knew we had a general with us, Grim," Thorkel said.

Grim said, "Don't send the slaves out. What good are slaves in a fight? They'd stand there and get chopped up. No, send out men made to look like slaves."

Ketil couldn't help grinning with pride.

"And kill the slaves," Grim said.

"What!" Thorkel was annoyed. "That's throwing silver away!"

"We can't spare men to guard 'em, and we've nowhere strong enough to lock 'em up and be sure they won't get out. You know we can't have 'em behind us while we're fighting."

Thorkel looked across at the slaves. "But that's—" He was trying to count, but gave up. "That's a lot of silver."

Grim laughed. "I'd rather be poor and alive than rich and dead."

"All right," Thorkel said. "Do it."

Ketil opened his mouth to say, no, they couldn't – but Thorkel and Grim were already moving away to give the orders. He looked at Ottar, and saw that Ottar's face was shocked too. But Ottar said, "It's war. We've got to." He ran after the men. Ketil followed.

Outside the church, Thorkel was ordering men to undo and repack the loads on the ponies. "Rip cloth up – use the slaves' clothes, they won't need 'em. Wrap the swords and axes loosely – so the wrapping will come away in a hurry. Fasten them onto the ponies with slip knots." That was a kind of knot that would hold the weapons in place while the ponies gently walked along, but would undo at a tug.

Having set one group of men to do that, Thorkel moved on to choosing the men who would be hiding behind the barricades, and giving them their orders. While that was going on, Grim had his own party of men, and his own work. They unfastened the Abbess and the nuns from the line of slaves and shoved them aside. Then, taking a man each, they kicked the men's feet from under them, pitching them onto their knees. The two warriors' heads were pulled forward by their hair, and their necks hacked with a blow from a heavy axe. One head was lopped right off; the other neck only partly cut through – but no matter. That man was dead anyway.

The monks were harder, since they didn't have long beards or long hair. But their hands were tied; and their heads were wrenched back by the nose or mouth, and their throats cut with a long knife.

The bodies fell, thump, to the paving stones and lay, shuddering, while blood pooled round them.

Ketil, watching, was filled with energy: he was jittery, twitchy. He wanted to fight someone! It came of great fear. At the thought of being chopped down as these men had been chopped down, Ketil was afraid, and his fear turned to anger. He would fight! No one would chop him into kindling wood.

The men, with bloodied axes and knives, turned towards the women. One nun ran to her Abbess, who raised her bound hands over the woman's head, and so embraced her, as if she could save her. The other nun, her tied hands at her face, sank to her knees, staring at the bodies and blood.

Ketil ran to Grim, jumping over a spreading pool of blood. He said, "Leave them. What harm are they going to do anybody?"

Grim breathed hard, from the effort of killing the men. He wiped blood from his face, and grinned. "There's many a dead man who thought a woman couldn't do him any harm."

"Tie them to something heavy!" Ketil said. "Tie their hands and feet! But – those two – are worth…" He counted frantically in his head. "Twenty-four ounces of silver! And Thor knows how much you'll get for the Abbess in ransom!"

Grim drew a deep breath, while staring at the shaking women. Ketil could see their shaking from where he stood; tremors of terror that made their bodies dance.

"I was ordered—" Grim began, but then wiped at

his face again, and said, "Hog-tie them! Make sure they can't get loose." Maybe he was swayed by the thought of the silver; maybe he just preferred not to kill the women.

Three of the men, bloodied weapons still in hand, went to do as ordered. The kneeling nun crawled away from them, but one dragged her up by the arm. The nun in the Abbess's arms shrilled like a rabbit in a snare, in a terror that turned Ketil cold. The Abbess's face was white. They were all hustled into the kitchen building.

Thorkel had chosen his men, and had sent about half of them away, to hide behind the barricades.

"You two," he said to Ottar and Ketil. "You're going to be nuns!"

They looked at each other. Some of the men grinned, but no one laughed. They were too close to the fight.

"They'll be expecting to see prisoners, aye?" Thorkel said. "So we'll let them see prisoners. Find one of those frocks – or a woman's cloak."

"Ketil makes a lanky woman," Grim said.

"So he'll stoop! It's got to look like we're leaving with our slaves, aye?"

One of the men had been unpacking something

from a pony, and now handed Ketil a fine woman's cloak. It was made of thick red wool, with a deep, fur-trimmed hood, and a broad band of embroidery about the hem and shoulders. It had probably been the Abbess's cloak.

Another man handed Ottar a grey, blood-stained gown stripped from an old, dead nun. Ottar's face wasn't happy. "You'll need someone up in the rafters, to give the signal for our ambush," he said. "Ketil and me could do that."

Ketil wondered if Ottar was scared to fight, or if he just didn't want to dress as a woman. For himself, now, he wanted to fight. He didn't want to wait in the monastery, and then find out that the Saxons had won, and were coming to kill him. He wanted to go out to meet them, and fight them on his feet.

"Don't need anybody to give signals," Thorkel said. "You think the Saxons are going to come for us on tiptoe, whispering? They'll hear it back at the fort. Grim won't miss it, don't worry."

So Grim was leading the ambush.

Thorkel lined them up in the way they'd walk, on either side of the ponies. "Know where the weapons are," he said. "Know which one you're going to grab." He had them practise snatching at the weapons a few times, so they could be sure the knots would come undone.

It was plain to Ketil how easily it could all go wrong. If they fumbled and the weapon stayed tied to the pony – if the cloth that hid the weapons stayed tangled round them – if the men hiding behind the barricades didn't come to their help in time – if there were more Saxons than they thought—

Thorkel marched them towards the gate. They paused while the men in front broke down the barricades; and then they re-formed and walked out, through the gate, into the open.

Ketil's heart thudded as he held the womanish cloak around him. He couldn't see past the edge of the fur-trimmed hood. Would he see the Saxons coming in time?

He felt pulses and twitches running through him, making his arms and legs shiver. Let them come! Let them come and fight!

CHAPTER FOURTEEN
Being With Odin

THE PONIES' HOOFS PLODDED. Ketil, walking with them, felt light and strange without his shield and axe. The Abbess's cloak was heavy on his shoulders, but gave no protection. He lifted the cloak's drooping hood and peered from beneath it, checking that the axe tied to the pony beside him was still within easy reach.

The Saxons ran from the trees on either side, and formed up in a line across their path, shields on arms, spears or axes in hand. They whacked the axes against the shields with a hollow, drumming noise:

Blam! Blam! Blam! The noise made Ketil's heart jump. It reverberated in the hollows of his bones.

Thorkel yelled, "Bison!" Ketil threw the hood back from his face, and saw arrows fall from the sky. There were archers somewhere behind the Saxon shields. He grabbed for the axe hung on the pony beside him – but the pony shied away, scared by the noise, and by the arrow that struck into the turf at its side. The axe was carried out of Ketil's reach. He lunged after it, but the pony shifted again, turning away from him.

Panic and anger seized him. There were men and horses at his shoulders, trampling, shouting, but he felt alone, and unarmed.

A voice, insistently, yelled, "Here! Here!" The panic cleared a little, and there, in the confusion, was Ottar's face, and Ottar held out an axe. Ketil grabbed it with both hands.

In the din and shoving, with nobody sure what to do, they shuffled into line. Someone gripped a handful of Ketil's shirt and dragged him into place. He had no shield, but he had an axe in his hands, and Asved on one side, Ottar on the other, both with shields. Arrows were still coming. One drove into the turf near his foot, as viciously and deeply as it would have driven into his flesh. And he had no shield to hide behind.

The Saxons pounded on their shields and chanted, "Yield! Yield!" Ketil filled with a wild anger. It shook him on his feet; he shook with the urge to run at them and chop at them, be revenged on them for being there. Only Asved's and Ottar's shields blocking his way gave him the sense to stay where he was.

Thorkel, behind them, yelled. He wanted the men at the end to bend the line round, to protect their flanks. He thumped Ketil on the shoulder, and when Ketil turned, startled, Thorkel held a shield, which he fitted over Ketil's arm. It was wonderful how much safer Ketil felt when his hand closed on the grip, and the weight settled on his arm.

The Saxons yelled, thumped their axes on their shields, and came at a run. Ketil wanted, for an instant, to run the other way; but he couldn't, because Asved and Ottar were standing their ground. So he locked his shield with theirs, and waited. With every shuddering breath, he swung between fear and rage, and each made the other sharper.

The Saxons crashed onto their shields: crash of wood and a man's weight, crash of metal. Ketil staggered, felt himself falling, stamped with his feet and braced them against the earth, shoving back, with all his strength. Beside him, Asved grunted and pushed. Ketil glimpsed an axe above his shield edge – the crash of it hitting his shield was lost in the general din of yells and horses' squeals and shields bashing – but he saw splinters of wood fly. His mind filled with the image of fighting Ottar at home, play-fighting.

The weight lifted from his shield and he tottered forward – but the Saxons had taken a few steps back only so they had greater freedom to use their weapons, and now his shield was smashed back against him, bashed against his arm, bashed against his head, dinning in his ears, bashed against the shields on either side. What was bashing at his shield was an axe or a sword – a sharp, steel edge that, when it had destroyed his shield, would hack into him. That gave him the strength to shove back, and yell. He never thought of using the axe in his other hand, though he probably didn't have space to swing it. All he could think was to keep his shield in front of him, to keep it tight wedged against the shields on either side, and to shove the Saxons away. Inside his jerkin, sweat streamed from his armpits and down his sides.

A great shove at his left, and he stumbled to the right. A hubbub from the left, an outcry of voices, a clang and drum of shields and weapons. They trampled with their feet, struggling to find foothold and stay upright as their line swayed, and heaved—

Ketil's breath came hard. His muscles were strained; he was running with sweat. He knew what it meant, this shoving from the left. They were being attacked from two sides. The shield wall must break—

Thorkel howled, "*Bison! Bison!*" A cry for help. Where was Grim – where were the others?

The shield wall broke. A man fell, the shields parted, the Saxons forced through the gap with a resounding yell. Spear-points thrust through, axes hacked, swords – men screeched, toppled.

Ketil desperately held up his shield. The axe-shaft slithered in his wet hand. He turned, thinking to fend off attackers behind him. He felt something solid yet shifting at his back – another's back. A man, standing back to back with him, to fight.

A scared voice yelled, "Ketil?" It was Ottar. Ottar was behind him.

I shall be chopped, like the slaves, Ketil thought. *Ottar will be chopped*. His fear and rage joined.

A Saxon swung down an axe, bashed on Ketil's shield. He took the weight of the blow, grunting out his breath, bracing his feet against the ground, leaning back against Ottar, who leaned against him. He could feel Ottar's hard bones, hear him gasping.

There was space at his side – the man there had gone, was on the ground – the shield wall was splintering – light whirled in his eyes as a weapon flashed—

Ketil screamed, sprang forward, swung his axe. Whether he felt terror or rage, he didn't know. But he would chop them, hack them, before they could chop him. He would kill them all.

Cold air at his back. Ottar wasn't there. Space opened round him as he flailed and struck.

He yelled – felt the yell tear at his throat – but didn't hear his own cries. All sound – all the yells, bashes, splintering, scraping, ringing of battle-music – went away. Silence.

All the wild movement slowed and slowed almost to stillness, and he had all the time in the world to run, and to decide where his next blow would fall, and to aim his axe.

Even colour went away. Everything turned grey and black and white. In that slow, black and white silence, Ketil smashed a shield, hacked at the man behind it, chopped at a knee, knocked aside a spear. He had plenty of time to kill them all, they were so slow. And when they were all dead, he could go home to Shetland.

His axe stuck in a shield, and he knew that while it was trapped, he was in danger. He heaved and twisted at the axe, with rage, with terror, and it came free. The shield split. Yelling, he swung round on a man, blurred in his vision. The man backed away.

Ketil glared about him. He saw Thorkel, his face shouting. He saw that the shattered shield wall was forming again.

And then another rush of men, with shields, with spears. Grim! Grim's men came in "battle-boar" – running together in a triangle. Grim, with his shield and spear, was the point, or the boar's tusks; and his men, their shields together, were the boar's flanks. They slammed into the Saxons' flank, yelling, stabbing. The Saxons broke, ran.

Something thumped into Ketil's back, as if he'd been hit with a plank. His chest and outspread arms hit the hard earth, knocking the breath from him.

He struggled for breath, and rolled, to get up. A man was above him, black against white sky. The man thrust down out of the sky, and Ketil felt a blow on his leg, a kick. Then someone, with a roar, with a smashing of shield, drove the Saxon back.

Ketil tried to rise, but a weight pressed him to the earth. Cold streams ran through him, running up from his feet, up his legs, filling him with cold water. He struggled, trying to get his knees under him, but a strong band tightened round his chest, stifling him. Cold chilled and weakened him. He couldn't rise...

Twisting up his head, he saw men fighting, but saw them through a tunnel of snow. Cold whiteness closed in on his sight from all sides. The tunnel shrank and shrank; more snow, more cold, blinding him with white.

He thumped to the earth.

"Bison! Bison!" Thorkel had no breath, and stopped to cough. He wrenched off his helmet, wiped his brow, shoved a hand through sweat-soaked hair.

Around him, on the ground, were dead and wounded men. Those on their feet were either running for the trees – three or four Saxons – or they were stooping, panting. Some straightened, throwing back their heads to open their lungs, sucking at breath.

Thorkel, looking round, swore by Odin and Frey. They'd won – after a desperate fight – but they'd lost men; and they still had to get back to the fort. And the ponies had run away, to be given up, or caught again.

Grim, grinning with strain through his beard, wiping at his own brow, picked his way towards Thorkel through fallen men. Thorkel started calling the names of his men, to find out who was still alive, who was hurt, who was dead.

Ottar came close to him and listened, as men answered. Asved. Olaf. Harald…

Bjorn was living and called the names of Strider men. Hakon. Eirik. Ivar. Hrolf…

"Ketil," Ottar said. He shouted it out across the fields and through the trees. There was no answer.

Ottar searched through the bodies. In places, where the fighting had been hardest, they lay tumbled two or three together. He found a living, wounded Strider man underneath a Saxon, and yelled, "Strider!" When men came to help, Ottar moved on. He lifted a man's head, and saw that the white face was a stranger's, a Saxon's. He shouted,

"Ketil!" And felt dread when there was still no answer.

He found Ketil lying in a space by himself, face down, arms stretched out. The leggings on his left leg were soaked with blood, and blood had spread up onto his shirt, and into the earth around him. Ottar dropped to his knees beside him. Ketil didn't move.

Ottar took his shoulder and shook him. There was no movement or answer. "Ketil! We won!"

Someone standing above him said, "He's dead."

Ottar looked up and saw Grim. "He's hurt," Ottar said.

Grim crouched beside him. "His leg's nearly off. Axe. Spear in the back. He's dead."

"They stabbed him in the back?" Ottar said.

Tired, Grim blew out a long breath. "From what I hear, he was with Odin. Berserk. They wanted to stop him."

Ottar thought: *Dead?* He knew what dead meant. It meant lifeless, like a lump of butchered meat. It meant, gone to feast with Odin or Thor.

He wanted to say, *But Ketil was my friend, so he can't be dead.*

He couldn't fit "Ketil" and "dead" together.

"He's not dead," he said.

Grim sighed. He rose, went to Ketil's head, grasped his shoulders and heaved him over, like a heavy sack, dropping him on his back with a thump. Ketil's left leg remained where it had first been, separated from his body. From Ketil's mouth came a groan.

"He's alive!" Ottar said.

"His last breath leaving," Grim said. "He's dead."

"No," Ottar said.

"Thorkel wants us," Grim said. "Let's go. If Ketil's alive, he can jump up and follow us."

Ottar stood by Ketil, as Grim walked away. Some part of him knew that Ketil was dead; but another part refused to know it. Ketil didn't move. Ottar saw that he was being left alone among the dead. He ran after Grim.

Thorkel ordered everyone back to the monastery, where they could look over the wounded, eat and rest, and think about what to do. He was in a filthy temper, cursing at everyone. As they came up to him, Grim said, "Ketil's dead."

Thorkel stared. "The wee Shetlander? I'm sad for that." He shrugged. "Odin's will."

"He might not be dead," Ottar said. "He's been

hurt." Because, if Ketil was dead then he, Ottar, would have to tell Ketil's parents.

Thorkel turned on him. "See that man there?" He pointed to a limping Strider man. "Shut your blether and help him! Do it!"

Ottar flinched at the angry face yelling in his, and quickly moved to help the wounded man. As he stumbled back through the monastery gate, with the man's heavy weight on his shoulder, Ottar wondered if they'd ever leave the place. Ketil never would.

CHAPTER FIFTEEN
Homecoming

A YEAR LATER, OTTAR CAME HOME to Shetland in time to see the barley sprouting in the fields.

It was good sailing weather, so the *Wave Strider* was eager to press on to Norway while it stayed good. The ship stood out to sea, while Ottar was rowed ashore in the ship's boat. He stood on the beach, a sack and a chest at his feet, watching his friends row back to the ship. He waved, but the men were too busy with their oars to wave back. The Strider men could almost smell home now: they could think of nothing else. Ottar was already in the past for them.

The sack held Ottar's war-gear, and the small chest, his pay: gold and silver coin, rings, broken armbands, necklaces, crosses, ingots, all weighed out of Halfdan's treasure-store. He slung the sack over his shoulder, tying it with rope to his belt. Then he heaved the heavy chest into his arms, picked up his spear, and walked to the town of Lerwick.

He, too, was eager to be home, but now that he was near, doubts attacked him. He'd been away for two years. Were his parents still alive? And his home farm was so near that of Ketil's parents. Even if he didn't go to see them, they'd soon hear that he was back, and they'd want news of Ketil. He couldn't think of any pleasant way of telling them that news.

One thing he'd learned was: if you put off an unpleasant thing, it never grows more pleasant. So he knocked at doors until he found men willing to row him round the coast to the bay below Ketil's farm. He sat amidships, his cloak wrapped round him, his sack and chest at his feet. He wanted to think of the homecoming ahead of him, but couldn't keep his thoughts from Ketil. He remembered Ketil lying dead outside the monastery, and how he'd been unable to grasp that his friend could be both his friend and dead. He shook his head at how soft he'd been in those days. A year ago, but it felt like ten years.

Ketil had fought like a bear in his last fight, running at the Saxons, hacking at them, hardly bothering to defend himself. And the Saxons, amazed and scared, had fallen back in front of him.

Thorkel had said that Odin had fought with them, in Ketil's body. "He had no bearskin," Thorkel said, "but he was a bear-shirt."

"But he died," Ottar had said.

"Odin gives us victory," Thorkel said, "but we have to pay His price."

They'd gone back to the monastery, rebuilt the barricades, and looked after the wounded as well as they could. Thorkel had sent out armed patrols to carry in their dead, and to find the pack-ponies.

The Bison and Strider men had been wild with relief and victory. They'd lit fires, cooked food, and found the monastery's ale and wine. They feasted, and made the surviving nuns dance and sing with them. Thorkel had told them they'd better be quiet, but they were too glad to be alive to listen. In the end, Thorkel had shrugged, and given up. It was the first time Ottar had seen him unable to control his men.

"Odin is still with us," Thorkel had said. "He's fought, now He feasts."

"Odin" meant "The Raging One", and Odin was supposed to have given ale and drunkenness to men, as well as battle-madness.

Thorkel had set guards from among the most sober men, but there were no attacks, and the next day, before dawn, Thorkel and Grim kicked even the drunkest awake.

They'd taken their dead into the monks' sleeping hall, and laid them in rows, their shields on their chests, weapons by their sides. Thorkel had Ketil's body laid in the middle, with his severed leg put in place. Thorkel gave him a spear, "Because that's Odin's weapon, and Odin chose him."

Ottar thought that wrong, though he hadn't said anything. Sitting in the little boat on the dazzling sea, Ottar remembered, and thought: *If Ketil had any choice, he'd go to Thor, protector of farmers and family men.* He could imagine Ketil marching up to Odin's High Seat and telling Him, straight out, that he wasn't staying in Valhalla. No, he was legging it over to Bilskirnir, Thor's hall, to take service there.

When all the dead were laid out, Thorkel drove

a spear into the earthen floor beside Ketil, and shouted out, "Odin! We thank you for this victory! Here is our payment!"

Ottar saw other men holding their clenched fists over their friends: the sign of Thor's Hammer. He held his own fist over Ketil, and whispered, "Go to Thor."

They'd set fire to the hall then, and left. They were far enough away to be safe by the time the thatch caught and went up with a roar.

He couldn't remember the walk back to the fort clearly. There'd been too much marching, and fighting in the time since. He knew it had been hard, as they struggled with the loaded animals, the wounded men, the exhausted slaves. But they hadn't been attacked. There were no Saxons left with any fight in them in that part of the country.

When they'd reached the fort, tired and hungry, all the loot they'd fought and worked so hard for, was *"carried to the standard"*. That is, it was taken from them, by Halfdan's stewards, and stacked in Halfdan's treasury. The two nuns, and the Abbess who might have been a king's daughter, were sold to a Norse-Irish slave-trader. Their price went into Halfdan's treasury. The Bison and Strider crews might see a little of that loot back again when they'd finished their time with the Army, and were paid off. If they lived so long.

Once back at the fort, they had to decide whether the Striders remained under Thorkel's command. Thorkel suggested that Bjorn should become their new leader, and the Strider men voted to do that. Ottar had wondered whether to become a Bison man, as Ketil had done, but decided against it. When Ketil had changed his oath, it had caused such a lot of trouble.

One good thing – the winter-long quarrel between the Bison and Strider men had been forgotten.

Halfdan wasn't at the fort. He'd gone west into Cumbria, and the commander of the fort soon sent the Strider men after him. For Ottar, that had meant tramping over many hills, getting soaked and cold in a lot of streams and rivers; and sleeping on hard ground in the open, or in Saxon huts, where he'd collected Saxon fleas. He'd often gone hungry, and tired, aching in every muscle.

They'd reached the Cumbrian camp – a hill-fort of great earth banks and ditches. From there they'd been sent out to raid the countryside around. They would strip a Saxon village of everything it had – food, fuel, animals, blankets, tools, any weapons, brooches, necklaces, coins or other valuables. They loaded everything onto the village animals or carts, and hauled it away. The people could only stand and watch. What else could they do against thirty or more armed men?

Sometimes they'd left the people behind – after all, someone had to grow the food the Army would take next season. But sometimes – especially if the Saxons showed any fight – they took them as slaves. There was always good money to be had for slaves, and the camp always needed women.

There had been some bigger skirmishes, even battles. Then they'd stood in line, Saxons on one side, Northmen on the other, all holding their shields and weapons, facing each other over the shields' edges. Horns had blown, the men had yelled, faces red, eyes bulging. They'd bashed their axes on their shields to make a fearsome noise, to frighten the enemy and encourage their friends. Ottar had felt his stomach churn, and the blood pulse hard through him, turning him dizzy... He'd never got used to that drunken mixture of terrible fear and great excitement. Was this how Ketil had felt, when he'd run berserk at a whole Saxon warband? Was this fear-filled excitement a sign of Odin being near? But Ketil's war-fever had ended, in a few eye-blinks, with his lying dead on the ground, empty of blood. Feasting the wolf, feeding the ravens...

The trick was to fight knowing that you might be dead by the day's end, but to ride the fear and excitement like a wild horse, reining it in or giving it its head, as needful. Ottar wasn't sure he'd ever mastered that trick.

The fight itself was always madness, whoever it was against. The two sides might spend a morning jeering at each other; but once they charged, it was shove, hack, heave, slash, stab – throwing all your strength and weight into every blow, keeping your shield up, keeping your feet under the hammering blows, hardly able to hear for the bangs, thumps, shouts; gasping for breath, dripping with sweat, but finding strength for another blow, another shove – because if you didn't, you'd go down, and once you were down, you were finished.

Battle over, there was exhaustion, a trembling in every limb, but also a crazy joy because you hadn't died, and you weren't crippled. Odin and Thor and

Frey, Lords of battle, were still with you. There'd been some wild feasts after battles, even if the "feast" had been nothing but what some Saxon village had hidden away. Still, they'd make the women celebrate with them, and a couple of times they'd burned down the houses, just for the pleasure of seeing such a big fire; which always made the men laugh.

The men of the Great Army had laughed a lot. When you had survived another battle, with nothing worse than a cut to the arm or a bash on the head, then everything seemed funny. In quiet moments, it was different. Lying awake at night, or in the early mornings, Ottar saw how close he always was to death.

How many times would Odin give him victory, before demanding His price? The more battles he fought, it seemed to Ottar, the more likely it was that the next would be his last.

He remembered how keen he'd been to join the Army, how he'd dreamed of taking service with a king and fighting in his war-band. What a little boy he'd been!

Lying awake in the dark, with no one to pass him ale or make him laugh, Ottar remembered the quiet life on the farm. When he was paid off, he'd have the money to buy a farm. The feeling crept over him that he'd like a farm more than serving the greatest king. If he lived long enough to collect his pay.

One night, in the Leaf-Fall Season of Ottar's second year's service, he saw Ketil. Ottar was lying awake in the peat-smoke reek of the fellowship house. Ketil came to his bed, crouched beside him and looked at him, his face red-lit by the fire. Ottar had pushed himself up onto his elbow. "What do you want?"

Ketil had stared at him in silence, while Ottar struggled to remember whether Ketil was alive or dead. Ottar said to him, "Weren't you killed last year?"

Ketil stood then, his head bowed because of the low roof, and said, "You'll see me again on the day you die." He'd stepped back, and faded into the thick smoke and darkness.

Next morning, Ottar had remembered this night-comer as clearly as if Ketil stood before him in daylight. He couldn't forget Ketil's face, looking down, or his words: "You'll see me again on the day you die." He made up his mind then that, when his service was up, he would take his pay and go home.

He didn't know when the day would come that he'd see Ketil again, but when it did, he wanted to be at home in Shetland.

And now he was in Shetland again; and with enough gold and silver to own his own farm.

First, he had to visit Ketil's parents. Thinking of what he had to tell them, he felt as heavy as a stone sinking in the cold sea; but it had to be done.

The coastline was more and more familiar. Ottar's chest ached. As the men rowed him into the bay, with the light dazzling on the water, and the cliffs he knew so well, and the farm there on the headland – Ketil's farm – well, he couldn't stop the tears coming. They ran down into his new beard, and he clenched his teeth to stop himself sobbing.

They reached the shore, and Ottar helped the men to beach the boat. "Come on up for something to eat," he said. "I know these people. You'll be welcome."

The men agreed, so they walked up to the farm together, with Ottar carrying his belongings. Ahead of them, they saw people hurrying from the fields, running towards the farmhouse. Their boat had been seen, and the farm people knew visitors were on their way. Ketil's father, Arne, would want to be there to greet his guests, and he'd want to have enough men with him to handle any trouble. Everyone else, free-worker and slave, would find an excuse to go back to the farm, to find out who the visitors were, and why they'd come.

Ottar felt worse and worse as they came into the farmyard. He'd visited this farm so often as a boy that everything seemed both strange and sharply familiar – an odd feeling. Oddest of all was that he wouldn't find Ketil there.

He saw Ulfbjorn, Ketil's uncle, coming across the paved yard to greet him – Ulfbjorn, the man who'd taught him to use weapons. Some farm men were close behind him, in case they were needed. "You are well come!" Ulfbjorn called. "I am Ulfbjorn Ketilssen. And you are…?"

Ottar thought that Ulfbjorn was giving him a curious look, and half-guessed who he was already. "I'm Ottar Haraldssen, of Haraldsstead," he said. "Remember me?"

Ulfbjorn peered at him more closely – then suddenly stood back and looked beyond Ottar, looked back down the path that led to the sea.

It sent a pang through Ottar, because he knew

who Ulfbjorn was looking for. "I'm sad for it, but Ketil isn't with me."

"Ketil stayed on?" Ulfbjorn said. "Can we look for him next year – or this Leaf-Fall?"

Ottar thought of saying, aye, Ketil would come later in the year... Then he could go on to his own glad homecoming, without having to tell what he knew; and Ketil's folk could go on hoping to see him again. That would be easier for everyone. But somehow, it was as difficult to say those words...

"Have you seen Ketil lately?" Ulfbjorn asked.

Ottar sighed. If they hoped to see Ketil alive again, they would only be disappointed when he didn't come at Leaf-Fall, or the next year, or the year after that... "I am sad for it, good man, but Ketil is dead. I have some things he wanted you to have."

Ulfbjorn stood still. He said, "Aye. Come away in. Don't say anything to his mother and father. Let me tell them."

They went up to the house. Ketil's father greeted them, smiling, at the door. Ulfbjorn said to him, quietly, "It's Ottar Haraldssen, bringing news of Ketil..." and drew him outside the house.

Ketil's mother, who'd been warned that she had guests, came smiling to bring Ottar and his companions to the fire, while her daughters and maids offered them water to wash in, and towels. "Sit! Sit!" she cried, and brought them cushions, and fetched them food – bread, butter and dried fish.

"Don't you know me?" Ottar asked her. "It's Ottar, from Haraldsstead. I've come home!"

"Ottar!" she cried, and took his hands, stooping over him as he sat, to kiss his cheek. "How glad I am to see you again! What a man you've become! Your poor mother! She'll be so pleased! You must hurry along to her tomorrow, first thing – no hanging about! And is our Ketil with you?" He felt her hand tighten on his, and saw her glance at the door again, as she'd been doing all the time she spoke to him.

Her husband came into the room. The woman's eyes moved at once to his face.

Ketil's father went to the curtain that screened the family's private part of the house. His wife moved to go with him. Ottar could tell that she already knew what she was going to be told.

While Ketil's parents were behind the curtain, Ottar talked to Ulfbjorn, and to the farm-servants and slaves, telling them about the things he'd done and seen. It was something he'd imagined himself doing, two years ago – coming home and telling tales of his adventures to admiring listeners, showing his scars. But, without Ketil, it was much sadder and more painful than he'd ever thought it would be.

Ulfbjorn sat looking into the fire; but the servants and slaves listened keenly, asking many questions. Ottar didn't enjoy the talk. He kept listening for whatever was going on behind the curtain. He didn't hear a sound.

Later, Ketil's father came out, sat beside Ottar, and asked how his son had died.

"Odin was with him," Ottar said, and tried to explain about the fight at the monastery, but he wasn't sure if Ketil's father was listening. "The Saxons were winning, I think... And then Ketil ran bersek. He and Odin won that fight for us, but...when it was all over, we found Ketil lying dead."

Ottar untied the sack that held his gear. Ketil's father sat watching, too caught up in thoughts of his son to care much what Ottar was doing. Ottar took a leather bag from his sack and passed it to Arne. "Ketil had a good friend named Thorkel Do-It, and when he heard that I was coming home, he asked me to bring this to you."

Arne opened the bag, and pulled out a string of amber beads.

"There are some coins, and an arm-ring too," Ottar said. "They're just a few things Ketil picked up. Thorkel Do-It told me to say that, when he and his men are paid off, they'll bring you his pay on their way home to Norway. You can be sure he'll do it."

Arne said, "Weren't you on the same ship?"

Ottar shook his head.

"How's that, then?"

"Oh... We had a quarrel. But for all that, he saved my life – I'll tell you about that if you want to hear it. He was a good friend to me, and I wish he was with us still. And – if you'll let me – I'd like to have a stone raised to him."

Ketil's father thought for a moment, then nodded. "Aye. His mother would like that."

The stone was raised a year later, on the hillside above the farm, looking down over the fields to the sea. It was carved with the figure of an armed man, and around the edge, in runes, it said, "Ottar raised this stone to his brother, Ketil, who fought and died in the Saxon lands with Halfdan."

Ottar went to see the stone raised, and stood with

Arne Ketilssen and his wife, watching the stone-carver's men pack earth around the stone, to make it stand.

Afterwards, when the others had gone, Ottar put his hand on the stone and said, "Ketil, whether you're with Odin or Thor, rest. Be in no hurry to see me again! I'm clearing my farm, Ketil, and your father says I can marry your sister, Asa. I'll name my first son Ottar, but my second I'll call Ketil."

A skirmish of rain blew in from the sea, and he could take that for an answer if he chose.

ABOUT THE AUTHOR

Susan Price is the author of over fifty books. She is the winner of the Carnegie Medal and the *Guardian* Children's Fiction Award.

Susan's passion for the Vikings has led her to Scandinavia to see the Gokstad ship, and many of her books are about the Viking Age.

Usborne Quicklinks

For links to websites where you can learn more about the cut-throat Viking world, find out what it was like to live as a Viking warrior and take part in a Viking raid, go to the Usborne Quicklinks Website at www.usborne- quicklinks.com and enter the keywords "feasting the wolf".

Internet safety
When using the internet, make sure you follow these safety guidelines:

- Ask an adult's permission before using the internet.
- Never give out personal information, such as your name, address or telephone number.
- If a website asks you to type in your name or e-mail address, check with an adult first.
- If you receive an e-mail from someone you don't know, don't reply to it.